THE PRIVATE WOUND

Titles by Nicholas Blake available in Perennial Library

THE
PRIVATE
WOUND

Nicholas Blake

PERENNIAL LIBRARY
Harper & Row, Publishers
New York, Cambridge, Hagerstown, Philadelphia, San Francisco
London, Mexico City, São Paulo, Sydney

A hardcover edition of this book was originally published by Harper &
Row, Publishers, Inc.

First PERENNIAL LIBRARY edition published 1981.

ISBN: 0-06-080531-5

81 82 83 84 85 10 9 8 7 6 5 4 3 2 1

To Charles and Sally

"The private wound is deepest"

The Two Gentlemen of Verona

PART ONE

Chapter 1

It is time that I told this story. I do not know if I shall ever bring myself to publish it; not because of hurting the people involved—those it could have hurt most are dead; but because it is a sort of confession, and I dislike confessional writing.

When I remember that marvellous summer of 1939, in the West of Ireland almost thirty years ago, one picture always slips to the front of my mind. I am lying on a bed drenched with our sweat. She is standing by the open window to cool herself in the moonlight. I see again the hour-glass figure, the sloping shoulders, the rather short legs, that disturbing groove of the spine halfway hidden by her dark red hair which the moonlight has turned black. The fuchsia below the window will have turned to gouts of black blood. The river beyond is talking in its sleep. She is naked.

I suppose it's because she still nags at my mind, because in a way she demanded so little when she was alive, because she ought to have some little shrine of her own (and without me who will remember her?)—yes, out of mere gratitude that I should tell the story. A story which, for me, began as an idyll, continued into low comedy, and ended in tragedy.

Not at all Eyre's sort of story, the readers of my novels would say. Far too romantic. They may be right.

But it is my story. And I wish it had never happened. I wish to God it had never happened.

I had just turned thirty. My first two novels having done

reasonably well, my publishers had offered me £300 a year for three years to keep me while I got on with the next ones. Together with a small legacy from my grandmother, this would enable me to give up the tutoring job. I wanted to get away, not only from it but from the literary pundits and riff-raff whom it was almost impossible to avoid in London.

My father had begun his ministry in the Church of Ireland at Tuam Cathedral. When I was still a young child, we moved to England and I had never been back to Ireland since. My father's death in 1937 set up a slight tremor of piety in me, and I decided to visit Galway, perhaps Mayo and Sligo too, as soon as I could.

" Piety " is a word which would startle my readers. Christopher Isherwood was my model in those days, and piety is the last motif one would associate with his earlier novels. I saw myself as one of the camera-eye school then: impersonal, sophisticated, ironic. It was certainly a reversal of rôles to find myself, in the West of Ireland, not a camera-eye but an object of intense curiosity to every eye in the place. At any rate, sooner or later a man feels the need to return to his first roots, and with me it happened to happen sooner than with most.

There was also the war, which even politicians were at last beginning to realise would soon be upon us. I did not want to run away from it. No, that's not true; I *could* not run away from it, any more than a rabbit can run from the hypnotising stoat. I just wanted a holiday from fear.

I could have taken it, decorously, with my fiancée Phyllis, but that she had embarked on a world cruise earlier in the year, with her mother and tycoon father. The latter might have been impressed, very slightly, by the knowledge that I was actually making money out of my last book : but news of it was still, I presumed, chasing him round the globe.

Not that I'd written often to Phyllis. An affectionate but so-far-and-no-further girl, whose image a few hundred sea-miles had considerably blurred in my mind.

It was assumed by all that sooner or later she (and her cash) would become my responsibility. But—I wonder how many others felt the same—the imminence of war was to set up in me a kind of irresponsibility, a potential recklessness far removed from my usual circumspect ways. Somewhere within me, though I little guessed it, was growing a lion which would soon be seeking whom it might devour—or be devoured by. The prey, the carnivore, against all predictable odds, awaited me in a small, dowdy little town in the far West.

After spending a couple of nights in Dublin, where I managed to pick up a second-hand car, I drove across Ireland, visited Tuam, wandered north to Westport, and then took the road back to Galway Bay: an aimless, restless pilgrimage. I had got a few addresses from agents in Dublin, but the houses they offered proved to be either too large or hopelessly derelict: the roof of one of them, a cottage near Ballinrobe, had actually been removed since it got on the agent's books. I was in no hurry. The summer was before me, and the Atlantic; and Ireland takes no account of time. I remember feeling fatalistically, as I drove south from Galway city, that I would recognise my destination when I reached it. There would be a Sign.

I had intended to stop that evening in a hotel at Ennis. But, as I ate my lunchtime sandwiches, I noticed on the map a name which had somehow escaped my notice before. I may have seen it on a signpost but it had rung no bell. Charlottestown. A few months before, I had read that formidable novel by Somerville and Ross, *The Real Charlotte*. And here I was, less than ten miles from Charlottestown. Was this the Sign? The novel is set in a different

part of Ireland: but I felt suddenly an odd pull to the place
—not the mild piety which had taken me back to Tuam, my
birthplace, but a strong senseless curiosity. Perhaps the
Irish in my blood had got to work already, releasing a drop
of the superstitiousness which normally I despised.

When I drove into Charlottestown, I dismissed the whole
thing as absurdly fanciful. The place obviously held
nothing for me—a typical West-of-Ireland town, one long
broad street running up to a cross-road and then down to a
river bridge; asses lying about on it; low, mean houses, every
second one of which seemed to have a shop window stuffed
with unappealing goods, on either side. I suppose it would
be picturesque enough to the visitor, but I had seen so
many scruffy little towns of this kind on my way here.

I was about to drive on when I heard an urgent knocking
in the engine. An ancient man, leaning against a petrol
pump, opened the bonnet, peered and fiddled for a long time,
then resumed his coma by the pump.

" Well, what's wrong with it?"

He opened an eye. " The devil knows."

" You'd better send for the devil then," I replied tartly.

The ancient man's mouth opened in a toothless grin.
Then he crossed himself hastily. " I will not. It's my cousin
you'll be wanting. I'm after minding the pump for him.
It's great petrol, they say. Will I fill y' up?"

" Is your cousin in the garage?" I asked.

" He is not. He's after selling a horse at Clifton."

" When'll he be back?"

" Ten or eleven, please God. He'll fix ya. Sean's masterful with the machinery. That's a lovely motorcar y' have,
and it venturing all the way here from the Big City. It's a
great driver you must be." The last two sentences were
touched off by the chink of money in my pocket. He pointed
down the street. " The Colooney Hotel. It's a lovely hotel.
My grand-daughter's husband's uncle is the manager. He

has a new bar installed only this year. Will I carry your
bags?"

"But——"

"Be easy. Sean'll fix it in the morning. First thing, I
give you my word. It'd be a desperate thing to drive on
with the machinery banging at ya like an Orangeman's
drum."

So, willy-nilly, I was condemned to stay the night in this
seedy township. The ancient man carried my bags, and
thumped on the door of the Colooney hotel. Nothing happened except the materialisation of a dozen freckled children in the road behind us. He thumped again, then raised
his voice in a screeching torrent of Irish. A young girl
opened the door, gave us a horrified look, and said, "Holy
Mother of God, is it a room he's wanting?"

"What else'd the gentleman be wanting, Maeve? Stir
yerself now. The best room. The one with a bath. The
gentleman is destroyed with dust, making a pilgrimage all
the way from the ends of the earth to visit the tomb of his
ancestors. And with drouth, maybe," he added, giving me
a bleary wink. Pocketing my shilling, he tottered off—
presumably to the newly-installed bar.

Unexpectedly, the room was clean and quite comfortable.
I had seen enough of small hotels on my way here to be
quite inured to the atrocious Irish taste in interior decoration
—I had little enough use for "taste" myself in those days.
Pleasant curtains and bedspread, in a magenta-rose-figured
material, clashed with an appalling acid-green carpet. Above
the bed was an image of the Virgin Mary.

I unpacked one suitcase, leaving the other locked with the
notes for my novel inside, and sauntered out into the town.
The children had moved down the street, and were clamber-
ing all over my car. When they saw me, they stared boldly,
then scampered off as I came nearer. Unlike an English
village in the mid-afternoon, Charlottestown seemed to have

its whole population on show: carts trundled past, groups of men leant against the house walls, women were ducking in and out of the squalid little shops, or gossiping with one another across the street.

One of the shops, just beyond the intersection, was a superior type—a combination of grocer, chemist and wine-merchant, with LEESON'S STORE inscribed above the window in gold letters. As I walked past it, a dark-haired man, youngish but consequential-looking, hurried out, gave me a preoccupied nod, and entered a solid grey-stone house a few doors down over the way. Pursuing this road, which ran at a right-angle to the main one, I found it petered out after a hundred yards into a stony track, with a farmhouse and one of those bleak, narrow Church of Ireland churches facing each other at the road's end. I had noticed the Catholic church as I drove in, on the eastern edge of the town. I turned back, walked east at the cross-roads, found the post office and mailed to my mother a lurid postcard of a Conne-mara cottage. Back again three hundred yards, to where Charlottestown ended abruptly in the bridge, a pasture and a bog. That was the length and breadth of it, I thought; a drab village with a pretentious name. Well, if Sean was as masterful with the machinery as his cousin had said, I'd be out of the place to-morrow. I returned to the hotel, followed —so it felt—by every pair of eyes in Charlottestown: as if I was a rajah riding an elephant down Piccadilly.

It was this sense of foreignness, isolation—of being a one-man raree show—rather than the need for a drink, which drove me into the hotel bar an hour later. The few occupants stared at me before resuming their conversation, in undertones. I ordered a double Jamieson. Presently a red-faced man bustled in.

"Mr. Eyre? I'm sorry I was out when you came. I'm Desmond Haggerty. I hope Maeve made you welcome."

He pumped my hand vigorously. The manager, obviously; the petrol-pump-minder's grand-daughter's husband's uncle.

"It's not often we get visitors so early in the season. It's a terrible thing, having your car break down on you like that. Never mind, your misfortune is our good luck. And Sean will fix it for you, sure he will, Mr. Eyre: he's a right fella with the machinery. What're you drinking now?"

"Well, I——"

"Not a word. You're having it with me. Padraig, another Jamieson for Mr. Eyre. The white whiskey, mind, this time. Did y' ever try Jamieson's white? You did not? Well now, drink it down. It's an experience. Slainthe."

"Good luck, Mr. Haggerty."

"It's a toilsome bloody journey all the way from Dublin, sure it is. You'd have a right to rest here a while."

I explained that I'd been touring round the West for a week.

"Is that so? And it's your first visit to these parts?"

"Yes. But I was born in Tuam."

His eyes popped at me. "Were you now? I've a cousin is a priest there. Father Ryan. We must have a drink on it. Padraig, set them up all round."

He proposed my health again. The other occupants raised their glasses. They nodded at me pleasantly. Why on earth should I have felt them hostile, or suspicious? They're shy, like animals: strangers have to be sniffed. Warmed by the whiskey, I was already gratified to be accepted into this company. An English rectory, public school, Cambridge, an intellectual's pursuits—they set up, in me at least, a desire to cross the frontiers, to come to terms with the life of the majority, even to share it. In every highbrow there's a Common Man screaming to get out, I thought.

"You live in England now?" Haggerty was asking.

"Yes. London."

"I was there once. A terrible noisy place."

" It'll be noisier when they start bombing us."

" You think you'll have a war, then?"

" I'm quite certain we shall."

" Ah well, God willing, it'll never happen," said Haggerty in a rather perfunctory tone. " And what do you do over there, Mr. Eyre? Are you in business, maybe? Or the English Government?"

" A sort of business. A one-man business, you could call it." I had no wish to divulge my profession. Be anonymous.

" A shop is it?"

" A very closed shop," I replied lightly.

Haggerty gave me a look, as if something had dawned upon him; and almost instantly withdrew his eyes, as if to conceal the enlightenment. Had I been able to interpret that look, I'd have saved myself a lot of trouble in the future.

But at that moment a woman entered the bar, and my attention was diverted.

I have been trying to recall my first impression of her. The woman wore on her head a cross between a jockey cap and one of those perpetual-student caps, which are in vogue to-day with the young of both sexes, cherry-red in colour. My eye was switched at once to the mop of hair beneath it, cut in a long " page-boy " bob which had been fashionable in England a few years before—dark hair with a gleam of red in it. She moved with a curious, rolling gait (pigeon-toed?), swinging her arms across her body. She wore a bright green, high-necked jersey and a very short skirt, rather like a kilt, of saffron. She was the first woman I had seen in a bar in Ireland, which perhaps accounted for the withdrawal I sensed in its other occupants.

" How *are* you, Desmond?" The usual Irish salutation, but not a trace of Irish in her voice, which was creamy in tone, countrified, but in a vaguely West-of-England manner.

" I'm fine. Is himself with you?"

"He was. Gone to the loo, I expect."

Again I felt that slight *frisson* among the other drinkers. Then a man came in, a little unsteady of gait—a large, loose, pallid man, with grizzled hair, dressed in corduroy trousers and an indescribably shabby hacking jacket. Everyone greeted him by name. At first I thought they were calling him "Florrie": then I remembered that Florence with its diminutive "Flurry", is not an uncommon Christian name for men in Ireland. He went into a huddle with Haggerty, who was now behind the bar. The woman sat down on a high stool near him. She gave me one quick but not shy glance, then took up the whiskey which the barman had poured for her unasked.

I noticed the large man pass a cheque, somewhat furtively, to Haggerty and receive a few notes. He glanced at me over his shoulder and asked Haggerty a question: I seemed to hear "West Britisher" emerge in the answer—not a term of praise, I knew well enough, in Ireland.

Though I have never suffered severely from paranoia, I had had one year of bad bullying at school and was still perhaps overquick to feel, or imagine, hostility. But at this moment, I remember, it was not so much hostility I seemed to sense as a personal isolation, like that of a man who has walked all unwittingly into a group of conspirators—yes, the atmosphere had become, in a way I could not lay a finger on more precisely, conspiratorial: the two men muttering together at the bar, the woman ostentatiously concerned with nothing but her whiskey glass, the fellows on the red-leather benches round the wall appearing, no less ostentatiously, to avoid one another's eyes.

The moment passed very quickly. Haggerty and the big man came over to me.

"Mr. Eyre, I'm sorry to have deserted you. I had a little business with Mr. Leeson. He'd like to meet you."

The big man took my hand, in an unexpectedly limp

grasp. "Desmond tells me you're staying in his lousy caravanserai, God help you."

"Ah now, Flurry," protested the manager.

"You must meet my wife. Harry! Forward!"

The woman slipped off her stool—a curiously liquid and graceful movement. The hand she gave me was a small one, and I noticed the delicacy of the wrist: she gripped mine firmly. Haggerty had faded away.

"I'm very pleased to meet you," she said, with an absurdly artificial punctilio. Her lips were on the thin side; she had used a lot of lipstick on them, not too skilfully. Her eyes were greenish hazel. I realised, with a shock, that she was something of a beauty. I remember getting from this raffish young woman—the discontented droop of her long mouth, the eyes that were set rather too closely together—an impression of some natural force either pent up or run to waste.

The incongruous couple sat down at my table. Flurry and Harry. Harriet, presumably.

"Well now, tell us all about yourself." That was Flurry, boisterous rather than inquisitive.

"I hardly know where to start. I was born in Tuam, of God-fearing parents. At the age of three——"

Harry laughed. Her teeth were very small and regular, very white too. She was wearing far too much of some all too pungent perfume. "Don't pester him, Flurry. He doesn't have to tell us the story of his life."

"Ah, get on! We don't have so many visitors in this God-forsaken hole that we can afford to leave them be. Do we now, Harry? Are you staying here long?"

I explained about the car.

"What do you think of the place?"

"It's a wonderful country. I don't know that Charlottestown is exactly a beauty spot, though. That must be your shop I passed——"

"No such luck. It's my brother's—Kevin. My younger brother. We call him the Mayor. He owns half the town. An ambitious fellow, Kevin. And what do you do, if I may ask?"

"I write books." It was out before I had time to check it. I could have kicked myself harder still for knowing it was said in an attempt to impress Harry. I looked round furtively. No one seemed to be listening.

Flurry's eyes widened. "A book-writer?" he said, putting a very long "oo" on the words. "D'ye hear that, Harry? Maire'd be mad to meet him."

"I shall call him Boo," announced his wife.

"Don't you dare! No, seriously, I don't want people to know——"

"Are you ashamed of writing books?" she asked forthrightly.

"Of course not. But——"

"So you're here to study the natives? Incognito?" said Flurry.

"No, no. I just wanted to find a quiet place where I could write my next novel. It's not going to be set in Ireland at all."

Flurry gave me a violent clap on the shoulder. "You'll stay with us then," he exclaimed. "As long as you like. We've dozens of rooms. Harry, wake up! Isn't that a powerful idea?"

It was an extremely disconcerting one. I'd heard all about Irish hospitality, but this was too much. I explained that I wanted to rent a cottage where I could be alone with my work.

"If it's money that's on your mind, you could rent a room in our house. What sort of a price could you pay?"

So *that's* what this hearty oaf is after, I thought. He must have seen my involuntary expression. "You could be company for Harry—two English in a nest of wild Irishmen. Never mind, though. If you won't you won't."

There was a pause, filled up with another round of drinks ordered.

"What about Joyce's?" said Harry unexpectedly: she had been silent a while, gazing into her glass.

Flurry slapped his knee with a huge hand. "By God, you have something there." He launched into an enthusiastic sales talk about a cottage, half a mile from his own house. Its last occupant, the widow Joyce, had died recently, and Kevin Leeson had bought it and done it up for letting to visitors. He'd not yet got a tenant for the summer, so far as Flurry knew. With a sly look at me, he added, "And I can sting brother Kevin for a commission, so we'll all be happy."

The Irish intuition, penetrating into one's secret thought and turning it against one—perfectly diabolical.

"We must have one on it," said Flurry, as if the bargain had already been made. He scooped up our glasses and went to the bar.

I found Harry's eyes on me, a long meditative look. Taking off the absurd cap, she shook out her hair. How well I remember that moment—the scent of the smouldering turf fire, the hideously ornate "modernised" room, the voices flickering and falling, and my sense that a charmed circle had imperceptibly formed itself round us two. She nodded slightly, as if she'd found some answer in her own mind. We spoke, together.

"D'you ride?"

"Why 'Harry'?"

"It's what Flurry's always called me," she replied indifferently.

"You're the last person who should have a man's name."

She gave no sign of being gratified by the compliment. "'Harriet' is so stuffy and old-fashioned. What's yours?"

"Dominic."

"My God! That's worse. It makes me think of a pi little schoolboy."

She was certainly a pert young woman.

"I used to ride a bit, when I was a boy."

"But you're above all that sort of thing now you're a famous writer?"

"Certainly not." I spoke with some irritation. "And I'm not a famous writer."

The faintest look of complacence touched her mouth. I was too young then to know how a woman may first try out her power on a man by rousing his anger, or that she will not do so unless she is interested in him.

"Go and get our drinks, Boo. Flurry's forgotten us."

"Not if you call me that."

"You *are* a touchy man. Dominic, then."

At the bar, Flurry was deep in conversation with a red-haired man. I bought the drinks myself and returned with them.

"Cheers," she said. "Who's Flurry talking to? Oh, it's Seamus."

"Who's Seamus?"

"Oh, he's our sort of bailiff. Seamus O'Donovan. I don't know what Flurry'd do without him."

"A fine-looking fellow."

"I suppose so. He bores me. Always telling us we're ruined, we've got to sell a pasture, we need to re-roof the cow-shed. You know."

"But that's a bailiff's job, isn't it?"

She yawned and stretched, showing her pretty teeth, the body beneath her green jersey. "Damn, now I've finished my cigarettes. Flurry," she yelled, "get some fags."

I gave her one of mine. She was always smoking.

Her husband returned with a packet. "I've sent Seamus to tell Kevin come along to-morrow afternoon. You can

meet him then, Mr. Eyre, and fix it up about the cottage.
I'll ring you here in the morning."

"He's Dominic."

"Who's Dominic? Oh, him. A quick worker, isn't she,
Dominic? Watch out now or she'll have you tied in knots.
C'mon, Harry, I want my dinner." Flurry staggered slightly
and brought down his hand on the table for support. I
noticed two fingers were missing. "Why don't you have
dinner with us?"

I muttered excuses.

"Ah well, I don't blame you. Harry's cooking is noto-
rious the length and breadth of the West."

"Shut up, you silly old man."

He lugged his wife to her feet, and turned to me. "Sleep
well. I'll see you to-morrow. Are you sure you won't come
back with us?"

"Really no, thanks."

"Good night so."

"Good night, Boo," said Harry.

Shortly after, there was an explosion outside. I could see
through the window Flurry, with his wife riding pillion,
weaving off on a motorbike.

"That one'll have somebody destroyed one day," said a
drinker.

"It wouldn't be the first," said another.

"It would not."

Chapter 2

Flurry Leeson rang me next morning. I was to come to Lissawn House for tea. "You can't miss it. Take the road south past the hotel. Then first turn right. Drive a mile till you come to the bushes. Our gate is just beyond on the right. Mind you close it behind you or the beasts'll be galloping out," he said, in between paroxysms of coughing. "Are you a fisherman?"

"Well——"

"I'll lend you a rod."

Flurry rang off abruptly, before I had time to tell him I'd not fished since I was a boy.

Sean had demonstrated his mastery over the machinery when I strolled along to the garage at midday. The engine was running sweetly again.

"I'm sorry I wasn't here to attend to you when you drove in, Mr. Eyre. Peadar's no use at all."

"The old fellow——?"

"That's him. My second cousin. They put him out to grass ten years ago. He likes guarding the pump for me when I'm away: it gives him an interest in life."

Sean was a bright-eyed, dark young man, with a trick of wiping his oily fingers on the waist of his jersey.

"I hear you're thinking of settling down here, Mr. Eyre."

"For a little, perhaps."

"You'd do worse than old mother Joyce's cottage, God rest her soul."

One had about as much privacy here, I thought, as a gold-fish in a bowl. Yet there was something rather winning about this fascinated interest in the stranger.

"If it's a holiday you're after, you've come to the right place. Mind you, all the young ones here are mad to get to the Big City, or America. It's no life for them here at all. But every man wishes to be where he isn't—amn't I right? Gerronoutathat!" Sean suddenly yelled at a freckled boy who was trying to climb on to the bonnet. "There's a bit of meat in the back, Brian asks will you take out to Lissawn for the mistress. His van's broken down again."

If the cars were unreliable hereabouts, the bush telegraph was in fine working order.

The sky had been overcast all the morning. But, in the temperamental way of Irish weather, the sun burst out after lunch and in an hour the sky was a bright blue, the far mountains violet, and the nearer land patched with brown and an emerald so dazzling that it almost hurt the eye.

I took the first turn to the right, on to a pot-holed lane which led between fields sprinkled at the edge with spring flowers. The land stretched empty before me, but by each of the few cottages I passed a collie was lying in ambush and darted out snarling as if it wanted to bite the tyres off my wheels.

The track, getting worse every moment, snaked about through the bumpy little pastures. I had visions of its petering out altogether and myself driving through an uncharted sea of green: but presently Flurry's landmark appeared— the track took a dive through a tunnel of high bushes, and beyond them was the gate.

A winding avenue of trees—mostly ash, I think—led me for about a quarter of a mile, and there at last was the house. I don't know what I had expected: certainly not this elegant, white building, two-storied, with tall sash-windows on either side of the door, and a bow window jutting out towards a river which slid along through rocks only a few yards away from it, to the right of the house.

I gazed at Lissawn House for a while, almost wishing I had accepted its owner's lavish invitation to become his guest. Then I got out of the car, climbed a stone stile over the low wall which separated the demesne from a strip of garden. Now I could see that first impressions had been deceptive. The brick path up to the door was ruinous: the door must have needed a new coat of paint for ten years, and the charming fanlight above it was partly shattered. Where once the bell had been, there was a rusty hole. The brass knocker looked as if it had lain on a sea-bed for centuries.

I knocked. And again. Silence, but for the incessant mumbling of the river. I pushed the door open—no one locks his door in Ireland—and called out, " Is there anybody there?" feeling like the traveller in that over-anthologised poem. Footsteps came from the back of the house.

" It's you. How *are* you? Welcome to Lissawn. The missus is tarting herself up for company. We have the Mayor honouring us with a visit, and his domestic chaplain. He'll be later than he thought; so he asked me, will I show you the cottage."

Flurry Leeson, in the light of day, looked even more ashen-faced. " I've a terrible hangover," he said. " C'mon now. It's only a step."

We walked out of the garden, along the river. Through a coppice, we came to a place where a spit of lush grass projected into the water. " See that pool? I got a five-pounder there last month. But the water's low now: we need rain. I thought we'd get some this morning. You didn't bring your rod over?"

" Well, actually I'm not so keen on——"

" Never mind, we'll fit you out. I've plenty rods."

Like many bores, I thought, Flurry Leeson pays no attention to what anyone else says.

"The house is called after the river, is it? Is Lissawn the Irish for Leeson?"

"I wouldn't think so." He winked ponderously. "Don't tell anyone, but the truth is I hardly know a word of Irish. A bloody awful language to get your tongue round. My great-grandfather came over here from Wexford and built the house. He was no scholar, but a great horseman. They say all Irishmen get concussed sooner or later but the Leesons are born concussed."

He paused to slap his thigh, bellowing with laughter. We were on a bridle-path which curved away from the river, and shortly arrived at the back of a cottage.

"Wait now while I get your key."

Flurry emerged, and we walked a hundred yards on. "Kevin has to keep it locked while it's empty," he said apologetically. "My brother is the one unconcussed Leeson. He aims to be standing for the Dail at the next election—not that half the deputies aren't dumb as haddocks. Wait ten years and we'll all be shouting 'Kevin Leeson for Taoiseach!' What d'ye think of it now? A jewel of a place, isn't it?"

We were on the track which led to Lissawn. A high fuchsia hedge screened the cottage from the track: above it, a fairly solid thatched roof showed. The cottage was newly whitewashed, outside and in. The door led straight into a room—two knocked into one, perhaps—the length of the house, with tiny windows on either side. It was sparsely furnished, in the usual atrocious taste; but there was a new calor-gas stove at one end, a sink, and a row of unused cooking utensils and crockery; at the other a table, two hard-backed chairs and an antique-looking armchair. Up an almost vertical ladder were two small rooms, a feather bed in one, a camp bed and a hip bath in the other.

"I wouldn't like to climb that with drink taken," Flurry

shouted up at me. "Has Kevin fitted it out all right for you?"

There seemed to be a sufficiency of everything. I came down. Flurry pointed out a good stack of turf, a pump, and an Elsan closet in the garden, the rest of which was given over to weeds, and an unspeakable rubbish dump.

I felt absurdly attracted to the place. "It might do. What's your brother asking for it?"

"That I can't tell you. But you need to stand up to him. He's a desperate man for a bargain: he'd sell his grandmother's skin if he'd a chance. What you want to do is put the comether on Maire: she has Kevin tamed. You should bring your wife out—you and she'd be snug as bugs in a rug here."

"I'm not married."

"Are you not? I'd have thought the girls would be stampeding after a fella like you."

"I've not seen any signs of it yet."

"Ah well, we must alter all that."

The enthusiastic Flurry was clearly going to shove me into marriage as well as his brother's cottage. He could not know that what attracted me to the latter was its isolation, the pure silence all round it, the thought that I could be happily alone there with the creatures of my imagination.

We walked back along the lane, through the bushes, up the winding avenue to Lissawn House.

We went round to the back. A weedy yard, outbuildings on two sides. Flurry called "Seamus! Are y' there?" A stocky, red-haired man came out of a horse-box. "This is Seamus O'Donovan. He runs the place. I don't know what I'd do without him."

Seamus wiped his hand on his trouser-leg and shook mine, giving me a shy glance. There was something guarded about him, I felt; he had a horseman's straddling gait and quiet hands.

"Kitty could be for foaling to-night, Flurry," he said.

The two talked for a minute. No man-master relationship here. I sensed some closer bond between the two.

"Anything you want, just tell Seamus. He'll fix it for you. Mr. Eyre's going to take Joyce's cottage. Did my brother come yet?"

"He did not. Clancy'd take the foal."

"He would indeed. But what'd he pay?"

The two men conversed again. Seamus shot me an occasional look from his very bright blue eyes. He stood at ease beside Flurry, who overtopped him by eight inches or so, in the attitude of a brisk adjutant with his C.O. A fumbling sort of C.O. at that: which made all the odder the way Seamus looked at him—a look of more than respect; I'd have called it hero-worship, if Flurry had not been so unlikely a subject for such a feeling. Or was it simply a solicitousness for his big, shambling, rather futile employer?

"Mrs. Leeson wants Fergus to-morrow," he said.

"Wouldn't you trust her with him?"

"I'd rather exercise him myself, Flurry. He's bold this time of year."

"She couldn't handle him?"

"She could ride the devil. There's nothing wrong with her hands. But Fergus isn't a woman's horse."

"Harry'll skin me if I tell her no."

"Ah now, she won't. We don't want Fergus destroyed leppin' stone walls, not just now, and you know if Mrs. Leeson saw the great wall of China, she'd have to be leppin' over it."

"All right then, Seamus."

I heard the distant noise of a car.

"That'll be them. C'mon, Eyre, and meet your doom."

I followed Flurry into the back of the house. We entered

the room with the bow window overlooking the river—a shabby, cluttered room, damp stains on one wall, a turf fire smouldering, a few lovely pieces calling for attention among the featureless rabble of furniture. Harriet Leeson was there already: a check skirt, and a puce-coloured sleeveless jumper which showed her upper arms to be as thick as a cook's—a curious contrast to the delicate wrists and hands. She waggled a finger at me, not taking her eyes off a trashy woman's magazine she was reading.

"What'll the reverend say to all that stuff on your face?"

"He knows I'm past praying for, Flurry," she said indifferently.

"Go and wash it off, Harry. You only do it to vex Maire."

"To hell with Maire."

Voices in the hall. Three people entered. Maire Leeson was a handsome woman; auburn-haired, high cheekbones, a scrubbed-looking face, large, slightly protuberant eyes. She was followed by Father Bresnihan, a middle-sized man with bushy eyebrows, hair on the back of his hands, and a pale, thin face in which very dark eyes glowed with intelligence or fanaticism, or both. Kevin Leeson turned out to be the man I had seen coming out of Leeson's store the previous afternoon. He was like a cleaned-up version of his elder brother, decisive, neatly dressed, consequential, long upper lip, long shark-like mouth.

Introductions all round. Then a moment's embarrassed silence.

"Mr. Eyre likes it, Kevin. Just the place for him."

"I'm glad. I thought you might find it a bit lonely, out at the back of beyond here."

"Back of beyond!" said Flurry. "Sure, it's only a mile or so from the thriving city of Charlottestown."

Kevin frowned. Evidently he had suffered a lot from his brother's clumsy teasing.

"You're an Irishman yourself, Mr. Eyre, aren't you?" he asked.

"I was born in Tuam. But I've lived in England nearly all my life."

"And you're thinking of spending the summer here?"

"Yes. If I can find——"

"Not a word more," said Flurry. "You've found it."

The others were looking at me. I felt like an article sent on approbation: I could almost feel Maire Leeson fingering it.

"I hear you write books," she said. "I don't think I've read any of them."

"I expect he's on the Index," said Flurry.

"You'd be wrong." The priest's voice was an extremely pleasant baritone. "I looked him up. I hope we shall be seeing a lot of you, Mr. Eyre."

"Tell me now, Mr. Eyre, what sort of books you write? Is it novels? I'm a great reader myself," asked Maire Leeson.

"I've written two novels." From her chair by the fire, Harry suddenly grinned at me: then her red lips rounded into a silent "Boo." I averted my eyes.

Maire Leeson deployed the usual questions—did I write with a pen or a typewriter? did I keep regular working hours? had I come to Ireland for local colour? I answered, very briefly. I had certainly not come to Ireland for literary chit-chat. She finally gave it up, a bit huffed, and—with a somewhat barbed glance at Harry's bare arms—asked her where she'd bought the new jumper.

The three men were talking together on some local government matter. No attempt was made to draw the women into the conversation, I noticed: Ireland was certainly, as my father had told me once, a man's country. I noticed too the deference paid to Father Bresnihan's views on secular matters—very different from the attitude to the parish clergyman in England. The priest interested me a good deal. He spoke with authority, with a calm assumption that, if there was a last word, he would have it: like a benevolent but firm father with his children. But, beneath this calm, I seemed to feel a temper held on the leash, or perhaps it was a capacity for spiritual torment: the haggard, ascetic face twitched from time to time.

Presently Flurry brought in a tray—tarnished Georgian silver, Woolworth tumblers—and put glasses of whiskey in our hands. Father Bresnihan moved over to Harry: Maire Leeson beckoned to Flurry. Kevin Leeson turned to me.

"Slainthe. Tell me now, what does London think about the international situation?" he asked in his self-important way.

"Well, I suppose most people were ashamed by the Hitler-Chamberlain meeting, but don't like to admit they felt relieved."

"You think war's inevitable, though?"

"Yes, I do."

"And I suppose the English say we'll be stabbing them in the back by staying neutral?"

"Some will say that, no doubt. You don't help things by throwing bombs at us in the meanwhile, you know."

Kevin Leeson blinked: his eyes took on a guarded look. The I.R.A. bomb outrages in England had started last January; and the worst were yet to come.

"What's the point of it?" I went on; then, seized by an irrational desire to shake Kevin's complacence, added, "Of course, they're only pin-pricks: but they've meant the death of innocent people."

"Ah, that's the wild men. It's their protest against Partition. I suppose they're trying to create a situation where Dev. will have to implement the ideals of the men who rose in 1916. Mind you, I don't hold with it at all, but——"

"'England's difficulty is Ireland's opportunity'?"

" That's true enough. Don't you think so?"

" I do. But I still don't see that killing innocent people is a good way of seizing an opportunity."

His face darkened. "And how many innocent Irish people--women and children even—did you kill in the Tan war? Tell me that now?"

" I know enough about the Tans, and the Auxiliaries. But two wrongs don't make a right."

The room had fallen silent. Father Bresnihan was looking at me quizzically: Harry had returned to her magazine.

" I hold no brief for the I.R.A. extremists," said Kevin, " but their objectives in England have been power-stations, and the like."

" Then they're madly inefficient. All they seem to blow up is pillar-boxes and bystanders."

" Well, Mr. Eyre, at least that proves there's been no collusion with the Germans. They'd have seen it was done more efficiently," put in the Father.

" I dare say. But——"

" You're a humanist, Mr. Eyre?"

" I don't think so, Father. Not in the theologian's sense, anyway."

" But you think we hold human lives too cheap over here? Maybe we do. But it's a question of values. When you believe the end of his human life is not the end of a man's life, your position is altered."

" You have him there, Father," exclaimed Maire Leeson.

" But that does not condone murder," I replied, annoyed by her sycophancy. " The Communists liquidate hundreds of thousands—sacrifice them to the future good of humanity. It's still murder."

" I agree, Mr Eyre. Murder can never be condoned," said Father Bresnihan soberly. " It can only be forgiven."

Kevin Leeson was studying me in a puzzled way. His brother rose abruptly. " I'm going to see if they're rising.

It's overcast again. If you've done with the fisher of men, Dominic, come and see a fisher of fish at work."

I followed him into the room on the opposite side of the hall. It was indescribably untidy. A pair of fish-scales on a table by the window, metal boxes containing casts and flies piled up beside them: tall narrow cupboards with rods and gaffs: a bureau littered with bills: five saws hanging from nails in the wall: photographs of dead fish and live horses: fishing nets stacked in a corner: a barometer and temperature chart: lengths of rope tumbling out of a drawer: an ancient radio set.

I picked up a medal lying half-hidden by detritus on the mantelshelf. It was the medal of the War of Independence.

"You were in the Trouble?" I asked, rather surprised.

Flurry winked. "I just picked the thing up at an auction. Would you care to take a rod?"

"I think I'll watch this evening, thanks."

Flurry lumbered out, with a quickened gait like that of an alcoholic who has a bottle in sight. We went to the grassy spit, a hundred yards away. The others were following us.

Flurry certainly knew his business. His casts had the feathery touch of a supreme pianist. The others had hardly arrived when he gave a leftwards flick of the wrists. There was a disturbance in the water; the reel whirred.

"He has him!" said Maire excitedly.

Flurry's whole face tautened, like the line. He looked ten years younger, a light of battle in his eye. The fish dived deep, then almost surfaced, darting, twisting, threshing. There was something sexual, physically provocative, in its movements as Flurry coaxed it gradually nearer the shallows and its silver belly could be glimpsed.

"Play him, Flurry, play him!" yelled Kevin, his sober mien vanished. "Bring him over here a bit! I have a gaff."

He struck at the fish. A last convulsion. Flurry turned to Father Bresnihan, saying,

" He put up a great fight, didn't he now?"

I was standing a few yards away. " Great fight!" I muttered. " What bloody chance did it have?"

Fingers gripped my hand for a moment. Harriet Leeson whispered in my ear, " Good for you! I hate it too. Turns me up. The hypocrisy."

" You must come and take a rod one evening, Father." Flurry was still breathing heavily. " It's an age since you fished this water. You can't be chasing sinners every hour of the day."

After a few minutes, we straggled back to the house. Kevin Leeson, an excited small boy no longer, fell into step beside me.

" You fancy the cottage then, Mr. Eyre?"

" It has points. How much rent are you asking?"

" Would five pound suit you?"

My face fell. " I don't think I could manage that."

" Five pound a month, of course," he said smoothly. Flurry, who was walking just in front, turned his head convulsively, as if he'd been stung, and stared at Kevin.

" For a long let," Kevin added. " It's about six months, isn't it, you've a mind to stay in Ireland?"

" Yes." I plunged. " All right. Five pounds a month." I'd thought he meant a week. He didn't seem the desperate man at a bargain his brother had made him out to be.

Back at the house, Flurry poured drinks for us. " No, I must be off," said the priest. " I'm glad we're to have you as a neighbour, Mr. Eyre. You must dine with me one night. We need young blood in Charlottestown, the way the younger people are all leaving us. No, thank you, Maire, I'll walk. I have to call in at the Cassidy's on the way."

When Father Bresnihan had left, Flurry turned a melancholic eye on us. " All the younger people leaving, indeed! And who's to blame for that but himself?"

Maire Leeson was up in arms. " Flurry! That's a

dreadful thing to say. Your own parish priest. I'm ashamed of you."

"Ask young Eamonn why he went to London, then. And where's Clare, for the matter of that?"

"It's a wicked lie! Isn't it, Kevin?"

"A bit of exaggeration, I agree."

"*What* is?" asked Harry.

"You should tell your husband not to spread malicious gossip."

"My dear Maire, I'd never dare order *my* husband about," replied Harry, with an innocent stare. Maire's handsome face flushed.

"If you're suggesting——"

"Ah, will you stop pecking at each other, you two," said Flurry. He turned to me. "The Father found Eamonn and Clare having a roll in the hay. He drove the girl back home with strokes of his ash-plant on her bum. And young Eamonn lost his job and had to leave the town. He's a holy terror, the Father. The purity of Irish womenfolk has him frothing with zeal."

"And why wouldn't it?" exclaimed Maire angrily. "Isn't he your parish priest? A priest has a duty, under God, to keep his flock from straying."

"He has a duty to keep his temper too, not go lashing out at young girls. Isn't that so, Kevin?"

"Well now, I don't——"

"The Father has a right to rebuke sin. *Wherever* he finds it." There was something in Maire's emphasis which stopped the talk in its tracks. Kevin at last broke the embarrassed silence by turning to me and asking what stores I'd need for the cottage: he would have them sent from his shop if I'd let him have a list. I arranged to move in the day after to-morrow.

Presently I took my leave. Outside the front door I turned left on an impulse instead of going straight to my car. I wanted to look at the river and the garden that bordered it at the back of the house. As I approached the bow window, which was half open, I heard voices from within.

"Five pounds a *month*! What came over you, Kevin?"

"I want him under my eye, that's all, Flurry. For a bit."

The two men moved away from the window. I could hear no more, so I returned to the car, baffled and disquieted by Kevin's extraordinary remark. I might have pulled up my stakes and left Charlottestown for ever the next morning: but, just as I was starting the car, Harry ran out.

"You left your cigarette case behind."

"I didn't," said I, feeling in my coat pocket.

"That was just my excuse." She put her head in at the window. "You *are* going to take the cottage?"

"Do you want me to?"

"Yes, Dominic."

"Why?"

"You will, then?"

Her cheap perfume blew into the car.

"I expect so."

"Goody. Don't believe everything they tell you." On which enigmatic statement, Harry waved and went back to the house.

Chapter 3

A week later I was sitting at my desk in the cottage. The fuchsia hedge blocked out the far mountains. My work had been going well, and I enjoyed the simple task of cooking for myself. Kevin had arranged for a neighbour to look after me, but one of Brigid's efforts had been quite enough, so I kept her now to bed-making and cleaning. It was nice to be off the telephone, to take long solitary walks over the countryside and an occasional drink in the Coloney bar.

Contrary to anticipation, Flurry and Harry had not encroached on my privacy. I'd had dinner with them once—a meal Harry ate with curiously self-conscious, gingerly movements of the mouth, as if she had a set of ill-fitting dentures. There was no complicity in her looks at me, and only a sort of boyish forthrightness in her remarks: Flurry kept up his usual flow of badinage. It was a dull evening. I can only remember two things out of it. I discovered that Harry was the daughter of a shopkeeper in a town on the Gloucestershire-Warwickshire border, which accounted for her countrified English accent.

"Harry's dad went broke. I picked her up out of the gutter," said Flurry, with an affectionate glance at his wife.

"You make it sound as if I was on the streets," she protested.

"Off a dung-heap then. Harry was working in a riding-stables when I met her."

And, just before I left, my tongue loosened with whiskey, I said to him, "Why on earth does Kevin want to keep me under his eye?"

Flurry regarded me quizzically. "Keep you under his

eye? Sure that's a queer notion. What put that in your head?"

I continued to hold his gaze. "You never know what's in Kevin's mind," Flurry said equably. "He's in Maire's pocket, and she's in Father Bresnihan's. I daresay they want to make sure you don't go round chasing the local virgins."

Harry giggled. "Boo couldn't chase a hedgehog," she said idiotically.

"Don't you be so sure," her husband said.

It was useless to press the point. Flurry did not intend to come clean. Or perhaps I had misheard Kevin's remark in the bow window. I left them, thinking what a slob Flurry was, and how infuriating was his wife.

This evening, as I tidied up my papers and debated whether I should dine at the Colooney Hotel or knock up bacon and eggs for myself at home, I saw Seamus O'Donovan walk through the gate. He'd been a great help getting me moved in and seemed well-disposed towards me: but he was still a mystery man—self-sufficient, shy, unsmiling.

"A soft evening," he said.

"Come on in and have a drink."

He followed me into the sitting-room, and at once sat on a stool by the window.

"Mrs. Leeson says will you drive her to a strand to-morrow. It'll be a fine day. She thought you might like a picnic. If you're not too busy with the book-writing." Seamus looked at my desk inquisitively.

"That would be very nice."

"She'll expect you at half twelve so. Your health, Mr. Eyre. You've not been to the sea yet." It was more a statement than a question. "There's a lovely strand beyond Tullyvarna, they say."

"You haven't been there yourself?"

"I have not. The sand's too tacky for galloping. It's an effect of the tides in it."

"Oh yes?"

"It's like walking in a nightmare—trying to run away, and you're hard set to drag one foot after the other out of the stuff."

Something in his tone made me look up, but I could not see his expression: his face was between me and the window. I gazed out over Seamus's head at the fuchsia hedge and the sky glimmering above it.

"It's a beautiful country," I said idly.

"It is. And a bitter one, Mr. Eyre."

"Bitter?"

"We've never got over the Civil War. It burnt out our charity, and left us nothing but bitterness. Half the people are still fighting it—with their tongues." Seamus's voice was beyond sadness. I poured us some more whiskey.

"Were you a Stater or an Irregular?"

"I was a neutral: Flurry and I'd had enough of it after the Tan war."

"You were in that, were you?"

"I was. From my sixteenth birthday, I was on the run. With Flurry Leeson."

"Flurry? I saw a medal on his mantelpiece. He said he'd picked it up at an auction."

Seamus laughed harshly. "He would."

"I'd never have thought of Flurry as a soldier. He's so——" I groped for an inoffensive word—"so easy-going."

Seamus rose to his feet and kicked at the turf fire. Sparks and an eddy of scented smoke came out. The blue eyes blazed at me.

"Flurry commanded a flying column in Galway. I was one of the Fianna Eireann—the Countess started them—what you call Boy Scouts over there. We ran messages. One time Flurry ambushed a party of Tans outside a village. What was left came back two hours later with reinforcements. They drove through the village in their Crossleys, shooting it up. Then they set fire to it. Two of our fellas was badly wounded in the ambush. They couldn't be moved. They were burnt alive in one of the houses. Flurry'd stayed behind with them. The woman of the house they'd sheltered in was driven out by the heat. Some Tans threw her back into the flames."

" You were there yourself?"

" I was. I'd run a message to Flurry, and the Tans came back before I could escape. I got a bullet in my leg. Flurry hoisted me on his back, when the flames reached out for us in the house, and came out of the back door shooting. That's when he lost his two fingers. I don't know how he got away with me—I'd fainted by then—but he did. He was a powerful great man those days, with a price on his head."

Seamus's unemotional voice fell silent.

" The story has a sequel?" I prompted.

" Flurry never forgot those men, and the woman, screeching in the flames. He found out the ones who did it. Three of them. He was gunning after them a month and more. He followed them. One day he and the column attacked their barracks. They brought out the three Tans."

" So?"

" They burnt the legs off them, then they threw the sinners into a bog to cool themselves." The innocent blue eyes gazed into mine. " You're shocked, Mr. Eyre?"

" It's hard to imagine those days. Everything seems so peaceful here now."

" Flurry was a dangerous man to cross, right enough. People think he's a burnt-out case now"—how odd to have heard that phrase first in 1939—" but I'd do anything for him. Anything, Mr. Eyre. I joined his column when I'd got over my wound. That wasn't the only time he saved my life. After that war ended, he was sickened of violence. You couldn't know what it's like to be on the run. Some of us it toughened, some was stretched too far. When I hear these brave boyos, who never slept on a mountainside or looked down the muzzle of an enemy's gun—hear them blethering in the snug about Holy Ireland and the Border and how the Big Fellow betrayed us and Dev. is dragging his feet——"

Seamus broke off abruptly. The hand that took up his glass was shaking. His sudden vehemence had almost startled me. The Irish, I thought, never seem so flagrantly play-acting as when they're engaged in the real and the earnest.

"Was Kevin Leeson in it?" I asked idly.

Seamus gave me a guarded look. "Ah, he's a great one for the politics. He'll be a deputy yet, God help him."

"In the Trouble, I mean."

"Maybe so, maybe so. I wasn't hereabouts then. He's a main-chancer, a manipulator, wouldn't you think?"

Seamus's obvious evasiveness annoyed me. "And is *he* a dangerous man to cross?"

"Sure, why should *you* be crossing him?"

The unsatisfactory end of that conversation was still echo-ing in my mind when I drove to fetch Harry the next morning. I knew now why Seamus stuck to Flurry so devotedly. I had a new light on Flurry himself. But why did Seamus clam up about Kevin Leeson?

Kevin, with his neat suit and decisive manner, seemed so entirely the practical man of business. But so no doubt had the Big Fellow, Michael Collins, looked when he bicycled through Dublin with a price on his head, wrecking the Dublin Castle espionage system and ordering his ruthless retaliations.

Collins, though—boisterous, moody, quick-tempered,

rough-tongued, loyal, with a quixotic streak—might not the young Flurry have been the same type? And now he was a ruin of a man.

It was a glorious day, as Seamus had predicted. The country had shrugged off the early-morning mist and lay stretched out before me in all its sweet colours. Harry was waiting at the stile, a satchel over her shoulder, and that absurd jockey cap not, I was relieved to see, on her head. She asked me how I was getting on in the cottage; she did not ask then, or any time later, how the book was getting on. She never pretended to an interest she did not feel.

We drove, with the hood down, into Charlottestown and out west. The road swerved and switchbacked over low hills: one strand after another, pale in the brilliant sunshine, showed to the right beneath us, with stone-walled tracks running down to them. A magpie flew across the road. Another followed.

" That's all right," she said.

" Are you superstitious?"

" Two for joy." I was aware of her studying me covertly.

We passed a cottage now and then; roofed or roofless, they had a derelict look. A man leading an ass, cleeves of turf on either side of it, waved to us.

" What a God-forsaken country!" she said.

" But it's so beautiful."

" It bores me stiff. You can have it."

" Seamus said you wanted to go to the Morey. Some strand just north of it."

" Anything to get out of the bloody house."

" We shan't meet him anyway. He told me he never goes there."

" Well, that's something."

" Why, don't you like Seamus?"

" The Lissawn watch-dog? Oh, he's all right."

" A faithful watch-dog, anyway. He told me about

Flurry saving his life during the Trouble. He's rather an impressive chap."

I swerved to avoid a collie that rushed out at us, barking frenziedly.

" *No!*" she said. " You mustn't do that. They never go under the wheels."

" All sound and fury, and signifying nothing?"

" Are you afraid of dogs?"

" I don't like killing things," I replied stiffly.

" And you an Irishman! But of course you're not. You're a West Britisher. Don't frown like that, my pet. It spoils your beauty. I'm one too."

After ten miles or so, the road degenerated into a narrow stony track, which writhed downhill, with hair-pin bends and occasional rises so steep one could not see over the top of them till one reached them. And then suddenly below us was spread a superb sandy bay, low hills on either side, rocks at the far end, and beyond them a peacock-coloured sea.

I stopped the car, to look at the map. The U-shaped bay appeared to have no name. We left the car in a field at the end of the track, crossed a shallow stream on stepping stones, and started walking to the sea's edge. The tide was right out. There were hoof-prints of cattle in the sand, leading away to the grassy slopes on our left. Far behind us towered Slieve Carvy.

The sands were as Seamus had described them, firm at first but then queerly clogging, so that every plodding step was an effort. Harry had taken off her shoes—she wore no stockings; her feet, like her ankles, were small and delicate. We scrambled about on the rocks for a bit, then climbed the grassy hillside which separated the bay from the estuary to our left. The stream we had crossed was running out to sea, hugging the side of the bay below us. A light, steady wind blew from the west. An upturned curragh lay nearby, supported on stones.

Harry opened her satchel: soda bread thickly buttered, slices of ham, farmhouse cake, two desiccated oranges, a half-bottle of whiskey. She seemed less fidgety now, less contrary.

"Tell me about your girl friend," she said presently, lying back on the sward. "Is she pretty? What's her name?"

"Phyllis. Yes, quite pretty."

"You don't sound very enthusiastic."

Well, perhaps I wasn't. But I was not telling Harry so. She pumped away for a bit, in spite of my lack of response: her curiosity about Phyllis seemed indefatigable. After a while, I found myself more at ease with her, talking freely, but feeling a perverse pleasure in over-colouring the picture of my fiancée, and at the same time conscious of a certain disloyalty to her.

"That's better. You're quite human after all. I thought you were just an old stick of a highbrow. So you'll marry and live happily ever after."

Something in her tone made me sit up and look at Harry. Her eyes were wet, little diamonds on the lashes.

"Aren't *you* happy, then?"

"No," she said in a very small voice. Then she began to weep, quite soundlessly, the tears welling out like a natural spring. When a woman cries, I still get a violent reaction from it: either I melt, or I turn to stone. In those days I had no defences against the unaccustomed intimacy of it. Phyllis was a stiff-upper-lip girl.

"Harriet. What is it? What's the trouble?"

"Flurry."

"But he's—surely he's not unkind to you? You two seem to get on so well."

"Oh, he does his best. But the fighting he was in—it ruined him. He's no good any more. Except fishing. And we're so poor. If only he wouldn't drink so much. I'm useless." Her incoherent words faded out.

"But you're a beautiful woman," I found myself saying. "Attractive, and——"

"Everyone hates me in this God-forsaken hole."

"Oh, come now, Harry!"

"They only put up with me because of Flurry. The great hero," she said bitterly. "They don't know what he's like. Irishmen have no use for women, except to breed from. You've got to be a mother, or a whore."

Her fingers were tearing at the short grass.

"Wouldn't you like to have children?"

"What a hope! He—we can't. I'm sure that priest thinks I use contraceptives."

What could I say? All this childish self-pity; yet it made me feel oddly protective—and far more mature than I really was.

"He's got such a terrible temper. You'd never guess it."

"Father Bresnihan?"

"No. Flurry." She had stopped weeping. Her green-brown eyes, opaque—like pieces of toffee, I absurdly thought—stared into mine. "When he's in drink, he hits me."

I must have looked sceptical. It had suddenly occurred to me that this woman might be a practised or a pathological liar. And on the instant she scrambled round, knelt close to me, and pulled up her jumper. She wore nothing beneath it. Her dazzling white body was covered with little bruises.

"Now do you believe me?"

"Harriet. You poor thing." My hand reached out involuntarily and touched her body. I was looking into her eyes now, and I caught a triumphant gleam in them. The next moment she had fallen forward on me panting.

Why didn't I take her then? I often wondered about it in the following months: I still do. I was not a virgin, nor undersexed. Harriet excited me tremendously. A man's perverse impulse to postpone a pleasure? The too sudden offering of that pleasure? The wish to master, not be mastered—to make the running? A residue of loyalty to Phyllis? It is difficult, perhaps, for young people to comprehend to-day: but then we were less frank, or less purely animal, about sex. A man felt he was committing more than his body to it, particularly if he had been brought up in a God-fearing household.

We tumbled and wrestled a while on the short-cropped grass. It turned imperceptibly into a sort of innocent trial of strength. Harry's arms were strong, but finally I held her, pulled the jumper down to cover her body, and sat beside her. She laughed at me, not in the least chagrined. We might have been two children romping on a village green: I had not even kissed her. But I knew this was only a beginning. No doubt she did too.

" You're quite strong, Dominic. For a book-writer."

" I don't like being raped," I said, smiling at her. " You do have lovely hair."

"Nicer than Phyllis's?"

" Much nicer." No cock crew. And I didn't give Flurry a moment's thought, while his wife and I kept up a desultory, teasing conversation. That was the strangest thing of all. Harriet's bruises had absolved my conscience, perhaps.

I remember I asked her about the Kevin Leesons. " Maire turns me up," she answered. " She's so pi, and always running with tales to the Father—when she has a moment to spare from breeding children. She's got six *already*! It's indecent."

I laughed. In her moments of gaiety, Harriet was so infectious. Her malice was clean somehow—unlike that of my London literary acquaintances.

"And what about Kevin?"

" Oh, Kevin's a dark horse." She gave me a veiled look, as if trying me out, when she said, " He'd like to make a pass at me."

" I don't wonder. Has he?"

" Wouldn't you like to know?"

" I can't think why you're bored here—the *femme fatale* of the whole neighbourhood."

" Maire keeps him on a tight rein."

" And he keeps an eye on everyone else."

" I dare say," she commented indifferently. " He fancies himself as a little Napoleon in Charlottestown. Finger in every pie. You know."

" But why's he a dark horse, apart from his habit of making passes at you?"

" I never said ' habit.' Oh, I dunno: he goes off on mysterious journeys, and he never tells even Flurry where he's been. And last month I overheard him talking to a man in the office behind his shop, and do you know?—the man was talking in a German accent."

" Well, that's no crime. Yet. What were they saying?"

" Search me. I couldn't hear them clearly. And then that old fool Peadar started nattering at me."

I looked up. The tide was coming in: the waves were already breaking under the bluff where we sat, and the stream was appreciably deeper.

" We'd better go, hadn't we?"

" If you want to. Oh! We forgot to drink any of the whiskey."

" I didn't need it."

I pulled Harriet to her feet. We stood like that a moment, looking gravely at each other. Then she smiled a secret smile and came into my arms.

Her lips were unbelievably soft, with a taste of the salt spray on them, and her breath sweet. Her tongue, like a little fish, darted and wavered inside my mouth. I'd never known such delight till now. We must have been kissing a long time, for I was awoken from my trance by Harriet looking over my shoulder and then pushing me gently away.

" If we're going across the strand, we must start now."

We scrambled down, on to the sand. The river was deep now. " You can give me a piggy back, darling."

The water came up to my thighs, and in the middle there was a patch of what felt like quicksand, but we got through and I put her down.

" Your trousers are soaking."

" Who cares? Good lord, what on earth's that?"

Down the hillside to our right a procession was moving. After the solitude and silence of the empty bay, it came as something unnatural.

As it debouched on to the strand, I saw that it consisted of about twenty men, all in black. The object carried by those at the front, which I had mistaken for a curragh, was a coffin. At the head of the procession, as it re-formed on the strand's edge, stood Father Bresnihan. Harriet gripped my arm painfully, shivering. I could see a cottage, half hidden in a fold of the hills above us to the right, and in the distance, parked near my own car, I could now make out another vehicle, a hearse.

" Why are they bringing it this way?"

" There's no road from the cottage, I suppose."

Harry and I were both whispering.

" But the river. Are they going to swim across it?"

No. There must have been a ford at that point; for the cortège splashed across and set off over the strand, plodding through the sand at a purposeful, short-stepped pace. Not a word had been spoken. I could not even hear the men's footsteps. The whole thing was incredibly bizarre: they might have been a troop of ghosts.

" The Irish love funerals," whispered Harry, still clinging to my arm.

The cortège made a detour round a shallow, saucer-shaped depression in the sand, a hundred yards away from us. It receded into the distance, still at that plodding quick-step, splashed over the river where we had crossed it on stepping-stones, and stood around the hearse with heads bowed while the coffin was slid into it. Behind us the waves sounded louder, stealthily encroaching upon the strand.

"D'you think Father Bresnihan saw us?" I asked, thinking of our linked arms and her reputation.

"Don't be so wet."

The hearse bumped on to the stony track. The mourners formed up behind it, and the cortège moved off up the hill. My eyes followed the black-clothed figures till they disappeared round a last bend. The afternoon sun was declining: the rugged stone walls up the hillside were touched with gold.

"Are you scared of the Father?"

"No. But——"

"He's only a man. Like the rest of you."

"Aren't you a Catholic, Harry?"

"No. Our children would have to be, if——"

"We'd better be going, hadn't we?"

"If you want to drive for miles behind them. They'll spread out, right across the road. They don't like you to overtake a funeral cortège in Ireland. Disrespectful to the dead."

We were sauntering across the strand. The satchel swung from her hand, and a rising wind blew Harry's dark hair over her face: the sunlight fetched glints of red from it. Her right hand as in mine.

We skirted the shallow depression, and found ourselves on a dune of firmer sand, with sparse clumps of wiry grass dotted about on it, and a little cache of bones where a sheep had lain down and died. Out at the sea's edge a flock of terns flashed and gyrated, like a mobile gone mad. There was a screaming of gulls.

Harry put her arms round my neck, sank to the ground with a fluent movement, as if she was a wave-nymph drawing me down. How well I would get to know that liquid, yielding, compelling movement of hers! It was so utterly different from her rather gauche, graceless walk. I had no sensation of falling to the ground: it was like being lowered on a cloud.

Her saffron-coloured skirt had ridden up high. She was wearing nothing beneath it.

"I love you," she said, her eyes closed.

"Not here."

"Why not?"

I had a momentary revulsion, knowing now she had come out here to seduce me.

"The bay's a fine and private place, but none I think should there embrace," I muttered in her ear.

"Oh lord! Poetry!" Her body stirred under mine. "Don't you want me?"

"Of course I want you."

"Well then . . . oh, you are a cold fish."

"I want you naked."

"Take off my clothes then."

"People could see us."

"What people? You just said it's a fine and private place."

There were diamonds again on her closed lashes. I kissed them away, but new ones started.

"You don't love me."

"I do."

"Say it."

"Darling Harriet, I love you." My voice was so shaky I could barely control it. I felt like crying myself.

She opened her eyes, smiling into mine, a quirk at one corner of her red mouth. I rolled off her and put my head on her breast. It felt burning hot, like a fever patient's. There was a smell of sweat, delicious to me. Everything about her was delicious. A hand ruffled my hair, then tugged at it viciously.

"I believe you're a tease, Boo."

"I'm not. It's just that——"

"I ought to be angry with you, rejecting my advances. You're the first man——" she broke off.

"——who's rejected them? How many have you——?"

"Now he's jealous!" she crowed. "Dozens and dozens."

"In *Ireland*?"

"Aren't you an old sober-sides! Now *I'm* teasing *you*."

Oh that ludicrous lovers' badinage! It seemed to me then like a dialogue of angels. Harriet sat up, her hair cascading over my face.

"Tell me some more poetry. Go on with the one about the bay."

"Well, it's really 'The grave's a fine and private place'."

"What a morbid idea! Did you make it up?"

"No. A man called Marvell."

"I don't like your Mr. Marvell then. Is that why you wouldn't make love to me? The funeral we saw?"

"I don't think so. But it did give me a turn."

"You only live once. A short life and a merry one—that's what I say."

"'Short'?"

"I don't want to be a smelly old woman on two sticks."

"Darling Harriet! You are sweet."

She gazed at me boldly. "What's your Phyllis going to say about all this?"

"I daren't think. Sufficient unto the day."

Harriet jumped to her feet. "Come on. Time to be off."

But, three miles short of Charlottestown, we caught up with the funeral procession, still swinging along at that jaunty, indefatigable pace, three other cars now following it respectfully.

When finally we reached the Lissawn gates, Harry leant across to me, gave me a last kiss, and scrubbed at my face with a handkerchief. Then she made up her mouth, and got out.

"Shall I see you soon?" I asked.

"If you're good."

She walked up the drive, not looking back. I turned the car and went back to the cottage, leaving it on a little grassed patch at the side of the road, which served me as a lay-by. I entered the cottage, my head so full of Harriet that I did not notice for several minutes the disorder of my belongings. Someone had gone systematically through my papers, my books, the drawers upstairs and down, but had not taken the least trouble to conceal his search. It could hardly be Brigid, then. Some passing tinker? But nothing had been stolen. It was really very odd indeed; the local curiosity carried beyond all reasonable bounds. I automatically reached for the telephone to call the police, before I remembered that I didn't have one. What did it matter anyway? I sat down and gazed into the turf fire, day-dreaming about Harriet.

Chapter 4

I had started keeping a diary a few days before this episode. Fortunately, the unknown person who had ransacked the cottage could have found nothing in the diary to betray the situation between Harry and myself, and he certainly would not in the future. Because I had to omit any intimate references to her, I have nothing to tell me when or where it was that we first made love.

How strange it is, that I cannot recall this—the occasion when my physical enthralment began. Well, I suppose it began on the day of our picnic. But which of all the nights or days in a summer so distantly, so piercingly remembered now, was the first to find us naked together? It was all a blur, shot through with sudden gleams, mystery and danger and recklessness pressing upon its edges.

The next morning I walked across to Lissawn House. Flurry was leaning over the half-door of the stable, talking to Seamus within. I told him how my cottage had been searched.

"Did ye hear that, Seamus?"

"I did."

"Could it have been tinkers?"

"There was no tinker within twenty miles of here yesterday," came Seamus's voice.

"Besides, nothing was stolen," I said.

"What ails you, then? People have a powerful curiosity hereabouts."

"So I've noticed. I'm not worried. Just interested."

Seamus came to the door, brush and currycomb in hand. "It could never be Brigid," he said, looking hard at me.

"I didn't suppose for a moment it was. I asked her this morning if she came back to the cottage after cleaning up yesterday. She didn't. I believe her."

"You should se. She's an honest girl," said Flurry.

Seamus chewed on the straw in his mouth. "Did anyone else know you'd be out on a picnic with Mrs. Leeson?"

"No. Well, I suppose anyone who saw us driving through Charlottestown might have guessed I'd be away for a bit."

"D'you want me to ring the Garda?"

"No, Flurry, of course not."

"They might have been after searching the cottage themselves," suggested Seamus.

"Why on earth should they? Anyway, they wouldn't do it in such an amateurish way."

"Wouldn't they indeed! Clancy's a stuffed cod." Flurry went into a rambling story about how Garda Clancy had conducted a search for one of the hidden I.R.A. arms dumps.

"Well," I said sourly, "there's no arms dump in my cottage."

"Sure I know there isn't, Dominic. But someone might have tipped off the Garda. Some informer with a bee in his bonnet. There's a desperate lot of jokers in these parts."

"I wish they'd keep their melodrama to themselves then. I'll tell you the *kind* of person I think did it—if it wasn't just idle curiosity."

Flurry and Seamus looked at me steadily.

"Someone who wouldn't give a damn whether I discovered a search had been made or not. Otherwise, he'd have taken more trouble to tidy up after him. Someone very sure of himself. And he wanted to find out more about me: he wouldn't look through my *papers* for machine-guns. Any candidates?"

I caught an uneasy glance between Flurry and Seamus.

"Aren't you the great detective now?" said the former, quite amiably.

" I must be getting on with my work," said Seamus.

And that was that.

Flurry took my arm and walked me into the house. Harry was in the kitchen, sipping tea and reading one of her deplorable magazines. She waggled her hand at me, not even looking up. Did yesterday happen, or had I dreamt it? Flurry told her, at tedious length and with considerable embroidery, about how " Dominic had his cottage broken into by a horde of ruffians while you and he were canoodling on the strand."

For a moment my blood ran cold: then I realised it was just Flurry's typical badinage. I think that was the first moment when a covert excitement blended with my depreciating attitude towards him—the excitement of the intriguer.

Harry manifested no great interest. " You'd better keep your door locked," was all she said.

" Oh, I've nothing worth taking."

At that, she gave me a long look, her lip curling up at one corner. A shameless look. Surely even Flurry would notice it? But he was pottering about the kitchen, gazing in a lack-lustre way at the tins on a shelf.

" Haven't you anything to do, you old fool?" asked his wife.

" Will you listen, the way she talks to me?" Flurry's tone was affectionate. " Sitting on her fanny there like the Queen of Sheba!"

I was acutely embarrassed. The telephone rang and Flurry shambled out to it. Harriet was out of her chair, lacing her arms round my neck. I could not shake her off.

" Not here. For God's sake!" I muttered.

She pouted. " Hell's bells and buckets of blood! Don't you ever say anything but ' not here '?"

She released me and pinched my bottom with a violence that made me yelp. I seized her hand and bent it back till she was kneeling in front of me. Bucolic horse-play. If my intellectual friends in London had seen it!

Flurry's steps were returning along the passage. Harry and I were sitting decorously when he entered.

"That was Father Bresnihan. He asked will you have supper with him to-morrow. I said you would. You're not doing anything else, are you?"

The Father's housekeeper showed me into the study. "Make yourself at home, Mr. Eyre. Father Bresnihan'll be with you in a minute."

A prie-dieu, a crucifix. Two walls lined with books, a third with filing cabinets. A shabby sofa and two armchairs facing the turf fire. A table in the middle, stacks of papers neatly arranged upon it. The room was more like an office than a study. In spite of the fire, I felt cold in it. I had only a minute to glance at the books—pastoral theology, philosophy, several histories of Ireland, 19th century novels —when the Father came in, with a tray holding a sherry decanter and two glasses. He poured out for me, gave the fire a kick, lit a cigarette (he smoked incessantly all the evening), inquired how I was getting on in the cottage.

"I hope Kathleen'll have something nice for us. I'd thought of taking you out to the Colooney. They say in Dublin you can always tell a good hotel by the number of priests you'll find eating there." His worried, ascetic face broke into a smile. "I seldom eat at the Colooney."

"You have delicious sherry."

"Kevin Leeson gets it for me. A professor at Maynooth introduced me to it, years ago."

"Kevin seems a universal provider. He's been very kind to me about the cottage."

"I'm glad to hear that. And you find you can work well there?"

"Yes, indeed."

"I envy you, being able to concentrate upon the one thing." He waved an arm at the filing cabinet. "A parish priest has to be an educator, a business man, a charity organiser and the dear knows what else, besides a spiritual director. Just now I'm trying to raise funds for a new school. It's a shocking poor part of the country, out here."

"But surely the Government——"

"The Minister of Education is a good Catholic. But we do not look upon schools and teaching as a purely secular matter. You think that a very reactionary point of view, don't you now?"

"Well, yes. A bit."

One could not evade Father Bresnihan's intelligent eyes, or mistake his sincerity. He was still making out a cogent case for the part the Church played in education, when we were called in to dinner. The saddle of lamb was delicious, the potatoes admirably cooked, the greens a revolting colour, between brown and mauve.

"Don't touch them, Mr. Eyre. Kathleen has never mastered greens," he said to me when she had left the room. "I eat them as a penance."

The claret was certainly no penance. A young tortoise-shell cat leapt into his lap and curled up there, purring voluptuously. We got on to the subject of censorship. Father Bresnihan admitted that a large proportion of the most distinguished European and American writers had their books banned in Ireland. He deprecated the influence on Irish culture of "the slab-faced pig-breeders": at the same time, the censorship was tied up with a need to preserve the sense of Ireland—a nation whose way of life was based upon religion—"you would not give a baby a box of matches to play with. Our peasantry are primitive and impressionable people, therefore they are much more open than a more sophisticated community to the harmful effects of books."

" Do you believe a book can corrupt a man?" I asked.

" It can pave the way to moral laxness, Mr. Eyre. And the better it is as literature, the more dangerous it is."

I felt again, though I disagreed with his arguments, the Father's serene authoritativeness: he contrived, without giving the least impression of self-righteousness, to sound as if he had the right on his side.

After we had moved back to the study, I raised the topic of General O'Duffy's Blueshirts and W. B. Yeats' bizarre attachment to them.

" Willie Yeats always had a weakness for power: he's no democrat. But he'll soon see through that lot of posturers."

" It's a Fascist movement, anyway. It surely can't have much influence here. The Irish are the most unregimentable people in the world."

Father Bresnihan launched into an informed discourse on the origins of the Blueshirt movement in the Army Comrades Association, and the antagonism for it of the I.R.A. and the Fianna Fail party.

" It must all seem very small beer to you over in England."

" We know so little about the present state of Irish politics, Father. Do you suppose Hitler is trying to use General O'Duffy's movement?"

" That godless fellow! He might, he might. But de Valera is determined to keep the country neutral."

" While the Blueshirts and the extreme Republicans would like to get it embroiled?"

" I dare say. But I'm no authority on politics," he answered, smiling.

" Then you're the only Irishman who isn't."

" Ah no, that's not true. There's too much bitterness in the country still: but most of our people are sick of violence: they only want peace."

" The gospel of isolationism?"

"The gospel of building up a Christian society from the ruins of the last twenty years."

"But isn't it the duty of a Christian to fight against Nazi values and practices?"

"I think you'll find a great number of Irishmen volunteer for the British forces, when the day comes."

"But Dev. won't hand us back the Treaty Ports?"

"He will not. That would be asking for a German invasion."

Father Bresnihan poured me another cup of Kathleen's execrable coffee, and broke open a fresh pack of cigarettes.

"Is there any support for the Blueshirts in your parish?" I asked.

"Please God, there isn't. Not to my knowledge. The Bishop has spoken very firmly against the movement. Mind you, you never know some ambitious young fellow might not try using the movement for his own ends."

"Like Kevin Leeson," I said idly. The Father looked quite shocked.

"Kevin? Ah no, he's ambitious, but he's terrible down on that lot. What makes Kevin tick, you know, is rivalry with his brother. Flurry's the hero in retirement, but he has the glamour of his deeds still about him. Kevin didn't fight in that war, or the Civil War. He's a cautious fellow."

"Seamus calls him a main-chancer."

"Does he now? That's a little hard. Seamus is one of the last romantics: a hero-worshipper. He'll never admit that Kevin's doing good work towards reconstructing the country."

And lining his pockets, I refrained from adding. I said how hospitable Flurry and Mrs. Leeson had been to me. Father Bresnihan gave me a very straight look: I felt uncovered by it.

"I hope you will not mind if I give you a word of advice. Mrs. Leeson is a dangerous woman."

"*Dangerous?*" A secret exultation bubbled up in me. I tried to keep it out of my face. "Dangerous? But why?" It was the first time I had seen the Father discomposed.

"She doesn't fit in with our community here," he replied, rather lamely.

"Could that not be the fault of the community, Father? An English girl. A foreigner. Country people are always suspicious of foreigners."

"I'm aware of that," he said sharply. He seemed to brace himself. "I have to guard against scandal in my parish. Mrs. Leeson is a cause of scandal."

"But why?"

"Because——" But, whatever reason might have been vouchsafed, Father Bresnihan was interrupted by the cat. It had been lying peaceably on his lap: now it leapt with a screech from under his hand, and fled beneath the table. Its owner's pale face reddened as he bent down to retrieve the cat. "Poor pussy! Did I hurt you? Come on up then, you silly thing."

The cat's eyes blazed from its refuge.

"Well, if you won't, you won't. It's a rebuke for talking scandal myself, Mr. Eyre. Not that that was my intention, please God." He clasped his shaking hands on his lap. "I do not expect you to share my beliefs about mortal sin."

I put on a puzzled expression. As if I could not understand his implication! Had he somehow caught sight of Harriet and myself on the strand? But who the hell was he to discipline *me*? I said that Mrs. Leeson and I had been for a picnic, and seen the funeral cortège moving across the sand. It was clear, from the way he replied, that he had not noticed us.

"You have to be careful there. They say there's a stretch of quicksand in the middle of the bay."

"I saw the cortège making a detour."

We talked amicably enough about Irish funeral customs.

I said how moving I found the solidarity of the mourners, and how inconvenient the way they hold up the traffic.

He laughed. " And that's not the worst of it. There used to be a custom, here in the West, for the priest to sit beside the coffin and the mourners to give him money. The more money you gave, the deeper feelings it showed for the deceased. An emotional status symbol! Well, we're rid of that practice now, anyway."

It had been an agreeable evening, in spite of that one awkward passage. Father Bresnihan saw me to the door, his cat, reconciled with him again, curled up on one arm. I felt admiration and warmth for him. A good man, an intelligent man. He had every right to give me a warning: I could almost wish, in his company, that I was going to take it.

" Come again. God bless you," he said, his beautiful voice neither perfunctory nor unctuous.

It was two nights later, my diary tells me, that I was invited to Kevin Leeson's house for that repellent meal, high tea. The garden at the back of their square, solid house was a riot of children—which of them Maire's I never got round to establishing. She put them through their paces for me, ending up with a jig, herself playing the piano through the open french windows—danced with solemn faces, rigid arms and bodies, and feet that twinkled like leaves in a storm.

" Kevin wants me to take a snap of you with them. D'you mind?"

Maire Leeson arranged the group and photographed us. " They'll be honoured to have a picture of them with a famous writer. Won't you, children?"

" We will," muttered one or two, without noticeable conviction.

" And now, one of you alone, for my own album. Off you go, children. Your tea's in the nursery."

I submitted—graciously, I hope. However much he may affect to despise it, no writer really dislikes being lionised for half an hour or so. It's the recollection of it that disgusts him: like that book which was sweet in the mouth but turned bitter in the belly. I even revised my opinion of Maire: she was more relaxed out of doors, among the children, with a tress of auburn hair falling across her flushed brow. A typical Irish *bourgeoise,* but this was her domain—the province of motherhood.

The drawing-room we entered was sadly depressing, filled with a brand-new suite of furniture which looked as if it had been mail-ordered out of a catalogue. The room didn't feel lived in. I could imagine the Leeson children shivering through their music lessons at the upright piano.

Kevin came in. The blunt head, the shark's mouth. Preoccupied but affable. Here in his own house he seemed more noticeably to play second fiddle to his handsome wife. The table was loaded with an assortment of food—scones, soda bread, sardines, beetroot, boiled eggs, custard, iced cakes, pickles, ham and tongue—to which Maire assiduously pressed me. "You need feeding up, Mr. Eyre, after all those scratch meals you're having in the cottage. You're terrible thin. Isn't he, Kevin?"

"Don't pester the man, Maire. Sure he knows what's good for him. Let him be."

I told them I had dined with Father Bresnihan two nights before.

"You did so. He told me he'd had a great old talk with you," said Maire. "You must have discussed very deep subjects, the two of you. Books and the like."

"Politics mostly, Mrs. Leeson. He was very interesting on——"

"There's too much politics in this country," said Kevin. "The clergy'd do well to be discouraging it."

"Leave it to the politicians? Like yourself?"

"Oh, I've quite enough to do without——"

"But I heard you'd be standing for the Dail before long."

"Well, I might. They need some common or garden business man's sense there. Half these boyos are still blethering away about things that's best forgotten. We're starving ourselves, Mr. Eyre, chewing over our past history. There's no nourishment in it at all at all."

I sounded him about the Blueshirts—how they compared with Mosley's lot in Britain. He talked about the temporary alliance between General O'Duffy's movement and the Cumann nan Gaedheal party in the early Thirties. "There was a rumour they planned to set up a dictatorship if the election results went against them, but nothing came of it." Kevin did not seem greatly interested; but I sensed a certain wariness in him, as if we were on the edge of moving into dangerous ground.

"Of course, though I've no use for those fellas, I'll not deny that what we need in this country is order," he said, his shark's mouth snapping tight on the word.

"Now, Kevin, Mr. Eyre doesn't want to be running on about politics," said Mrs. Leeson. It always amuses me—the way women think they have a prerogative to say what a man wants.

"Well, Mrs. Leeson, I seem to have got involved in them, whether I like it or not. Someone made a search of my papers the other day."

"He didn't!"

"Searched your papers?" exclaimed Kevin. "What an extraordinary thing! D'you mean, broke into the cottage?"

"Hardly that. It's not locked."

"But it's a scandalous thing. Did you call in the Garda?"

"No. Nothing was missing."

"Well, isn't that a mystery?" said Maire.

It occurred to me that there was a mystery in the Leesons, at the centre of the Charlottestown grape-vine, not having heard about it. But when Kevin asked me what day it had happened, he said he'd been in Dublin at the time.

"Kevin's always running about the country on his business affairs," remarked Maire.

"Perhaps it was a spy——"

Kevin put on one of his shut expressions.

"—a spy from the Irish censorship, come to see if I was writing a pornographic book," I said flippantly.

"Ah, go on, Mr. Eyre! Sure you'd never do that, a nice young man like you!" Maire Leeson was quite shocked.

After which, she was soon embarked on a fervent declamation about the purity of Irish culture, the tradition of the ancient literature in Irish, the language revival, and so on. Names of old bards flowed out—O'Bruadair, O'Rathaile, Raftery, O'Carolan, Merryman. I knew now, from the way she talked, that she must have been a school mistress, and a good one. I had to revise my opinion of her as a mere culture snob. Kevin listened with obvious pride. It would have been cruel to suggest that the Irish language was a dead end for literature to-day: and this was no place to recall the story of the politician who perorated at an election meeting, "Irish culture owes nothing to Byzantium. Irish culture owes nothing to Greece or to Rome. Irish culture owes nothing to Great Britain (storms of applause). Irish culture is a pure lily blooming alone in a bog." (Voice from audience "And that's the bugger of it, misther.")

I contented myself with putting up a case for the Anglo-Irish literature from Swift to Yeats, as the greatest glory of the country. We argued a bit about Tom Moore, whom Maire regarded as a perverter of native folk-tunes. I got quite heated about this—I'd been brought up on the Irish Melodies. And presently she had fished out a volume of them and sat down at the piano to accompany me. I used to sing a lot in those days. As an accompanist, Maire was a bit wooden; but the Moore settings are absurdly ornate anyway.

"You have a beautiful voice," she said, after the first song.

"Go on, now," said Kevin. "You two get along famously."

But my strongest memory of that evening was glancing through the french window while I sang "She is far from the land," and seeing a huddle of children outside, in their night-dresses, staring back at me silent and rapt, the last light of the sun turning their ruffled hair into aureoles . . .

I suppose I remember that with particular vividness because of what happened later. How many days later, I do not remember: or whether it was the first time. That green spit by the Lissawn became a place of assignation for Harriet and myself.

It is midnight, with a half moon dandled by the rocking branches. I am waiting for her there, trembling with excitement and fear. I see her figure ghosting towards me through the copse. She is wearing a long white night-dress. We fall into each other's arms. I mutter something about Flurry: she says he always sleeps like a log, with the drink taken. In the moonlight her face has softened: she looks supernaturally beautiful. I take off her night-dress and my own clothes. We kneel up, facing together, our bodies touching, two white figures on a tomb, and gaze at each other. I want to hold the moment for ever. But she is impatient: she pulls me down on top of her into the lush grass, then lies passive.

The rocks of the Lissawn are sucking at the stream. A light mist rises from it, and in my body the sweetness rises —or was the mist in my eyes? is it only in my memory? For me, the wave topples over too soon. There are the diamond drops back on her lashes, and she sobs a little.

Presently, I enter her again. She seems passive, yet she

fits her movements fluently to mine. It is like swimming in nectar, her breasts and belly the little waves. And now her arms clutch me tighter, tenacious as garlands of white flowers strung on wire. I hear that familiar straining noise in her throat--she never cried out loud any time I made love to her—and feel her body melting, collapsing.

We lie inert, side by side, not talking. Two animals which have escaped from time and the fear of the hunters. After a while she leans over me, her breasts trembling, the nipples like buds put to sleep. She kisses me lazily, murmurs " good night," puts on her night-dress, and flits away from me through the trees.

Chapter 5

When I read it through again, I nearly struck out that last passage. Brute copulation hallowed by time. The coacervation of two mounds of flesh, seen through a moondust haze. But then I thought, no. While I wrote the passage, I became the young romantic I was writing about: dishonest to view him through disillusioned eyes: I am not compiling a textbook about sex in the West of Ireland. Rule 1 for the novelist—don't fall in love with your characters. But I *was* in love with Harriet. And with myself? Yes: a lover does that to one.

And what did she think about me? Goodness knows. She was a strange mixture of delicacy and coarseness. The delicate wrists and ears and ankles: the coarse, fat upper arms, the buttocks which felt as hard as polished marble. The absurd genteel mouthings when she ate; the foul language she used, the hobbledehoy teasings: but also a touching simplicity of mind.

"I'd been pure so long till you came," she said to me once.

"*Pure?*"

"You know what I mean." She blushed faintly.

I did. It was such an extraordinary word to use. Nor did I entirely believe her, for she had implied more than once that Kevin's pass at her had been followed through—though perhaps that was said just to rouse my jealousy.

She would be called a nymphomaniac to-day, no doubt. She was certainly insatiable. Yet, when we lay together, she used none of the experienced woman's verbal tricks to arouse me, none of that shameless, titillating love-talk. Her lust put on no trimmings: it was simple as an animal's.

It was only in public that she was shameless, walking with me through Charlottestown, jeering at me and wrestling with me, like a child, in front of her husband's eyes. I never ceased to be embarrassed by this. But I learnt to close that part of my mind which liked Flurry, and use only the part which had grown to think of him as a complaisant cuckold and a bore.

Did Harriet plan her campaign? I simply don't know. After our first flare-up, she would sometimes let a week or ten days pass before she sought me again; and if we did meet, treated me almost with indifference. Was it a calculated way to keep my desire on the boil? Somehow, I suspect not. And yet she enjoyed stratagems, the more outrageous the better. But then she would lose interest completely, become bored and peevish; and again I would wonder if she had it all worked out so as to keep me her slave, in a state of uncertainty.

One day I would think her a paragon of women; the next day, a whore.

During the periods she was off me, I was not unhappy. I had my book; and I spent long afternoons wandering around the coast with my field-glasses, watching sea-birds.

Harriet's recklessness endeared her to me—and communicated itself to me. She never used contraceptives, for instance, and refused to let me do so. She believed in the "safe period"; and anyway, she said, she had never conceived with Flurry, so obviously she couldn't with anyone else. It did not seem so obvious to me. But her care-free moods infected me; I was hopelessly infatuated with her, and not in the least deflected from my course by finding a note one evening late in May, propped up against my type-writer—

LAY OFF IT YOU HAVE BEEN WARNED

I am as cowardly as the next man, and I cannot pretend

this anonymous scrawl gave me no qualms. For a day or two, I felt paranoiac symptoms. But, when I told Harriet about it, she was going through one of her off periods and showed only the most perfunctory concern. Flurry, for some reason, I did not tell. Guilt, no doubt; but also partly because I could not believe him the kind of man to issue anonymous warnings. I used to wonder if this one were the work of the person who had searched my cottage: but what on earth was *he* warning me to lay off?

Besides, I was caught up in Harriet's recklessness, and like any young man wanting his girl's admiration, determined not to let her catch the least whiff of my fear.

And now the persecution campaign, if that is what it was, seemed to have been dropped. Harriet and I were together again. The assignations by night on the grassy spit recommenced. Sometimes she would walk over to my lonely cottage, and we made love on the floor, too impatient to climb the ladder to the bed upstairs. Wherever we happened to be—under trees in the Lissawn demesne, on a mountainside or on a strand, she would grip me with her delicately strong hands and pull me down. I was enchanted by her. It was a kind of madness. The sun shone all day, burst out from rain-storms and sent the clouds packing. England, my friends there, the imminent war, all seemed a life-time away.

Harriet and I went for some rides together. She was indeed a marvellous horsewoman and I followed her lead over banks and stone walls—as in other things—determined not to let her see me frightened. There was something gallant in her bearing on horseback: she seemed to me almost a mythical figure.

It was when we'd returned one June evening with the horses to Lissawn House, and I was walking back alone to the cottage, that someone took a pot-shot at me from the thick bushes lining the left-hand side of the lane.

The gun appeared to go off in my ear, so loud was the explosion. I had never been under fire before, so I stood a few moments utterly stupefied. My tall Connemara tweed hat had flown off my head. I bent down dazedly to pick it up, and heard footsteps pounding away from the ambush. There were two pellet holes in the top of the hat. The bushes are very thick just there, and I could not break through them even if I had the nerve to follow my assailant. But I was now angry enough to run back along the lane to Lissawn House.

Flurry was sitting in his fishing-room, a glass of whiskey at his side. I banged on the window and rushed in.

"What the devil ails ya, Dominic? You're white as a sheet." His voice was slurred, and a bit petulant.

"Someone's just taken a shot at me. From the bushes. Look at my hat."

Flurry's eyes focused with some difficulty. "By God, you're right! Did ye see the fella?"

"No."

He poured me half a glass of neat whiskey. "Drink up. This'll never do at all. Who'd be wanting to shoot you, in the name of God?"

"Search me."

"Maybe he was after a rabbit."

"A *flying* rabbit?"

"Well now, that's a point. But there might be some bold young sinner around with his da's shotgun. We'll ask Seamus did he see anyone."

Seamus was in his room above the stable, cleaning harness. No, he'd not seen anyone in the demesne, but he'd been rubbing down the horses the last half-hour. He asked me a number of questions, the efficient adjutant.

"Will I tell you what I'm thinking, Mr. Eyre?"

"Of course."

"If the fella was so near to you, he'd be apt to blow your head off."

"But he *was*. The explosion damn' near deafened me."

"So he must have deliberately aimed high. The charge went over your head, except for two pellets. That's the size of it." Seamus didn't seem greatly concerned.

"But why should anyone want to aim *over* his head?" asked Flurry interestedly. I felt like an academic problem under discussion, and said so.

"Why should anyone want to fire at me at all?"

Seamus regarded me politely, coolly. "Only yourself would be after knowing that, Mr. Eyre."

"Sure, Dominic is a quiet fella. He wouldn't be making enemies," offered Flurry. I hardly heard him. Had Seamus hinted at something? Involuntarily, my eyes went round the room. There was no shotgun to be seen; and I could hardly search the outbuildings and demesne in case Seamus had dumped it somewhere.

"You're not frit, Mr. Eyre?" he said. "Will I walk back with you?"

"Oh, I'm scared stiff. I'll go to the Garda to-morrow and demand police protection," I replied satirically. I thought I saw a look of respect in Seamus's eyes.

"That's the boy," said Flurry tipsily. "To hell with them all. C'mon and have a bite to eat. Harry'll be done bathing by now. I don't know why that woman's got so desperate to take baths nowadays."

I declined his invitation politely. The next morning I went to the Garda in Charlottestown and had a long conversation with a somewhat incredulous sergeant.

"Well, I didn't blow two holes in this hat myself," I said after a while, exasperated by the slow-motion talk.

"Sure you didn't," replied the sergeant soothingly. "We'll look into it."

"And I'm talking about my hat, not through it."

He thought this extremely witty. "That's a good one! I must tell the inspector. Are you over here for long? D'you like the country?"

"Very much. Except when I'm taken for a pheasant."

"You have it, Mr. Eyre! The boys do a terrible lot of poaching round here. Yes, the fella must have been aiming at a bird."

"Let's hope so. But there were no birds about."

"Were there not? How d'you know?"

"I use my eyes."

"And them great field-glasses, so I hear."

"Yes. I like bird-watching." So I'd even been under observation by the police.

"You're an ornithologist, Mr. Eyre?"

"No. Just a bird-watcher."

There was a puzzled expression on his face, but he let it pass. I debated whether to tell him about the search of my cottage: perhaps unwisely, I decided not to increase his confusion, or suspicion, or whatever it was. We parted with expressions of mutual esteem.

Getting into my car down the road, I was hailed by Father Bresnihan. He leapt off his bike beside me, his thick eyebrows and burning eyes came very close to me. "So you didn't take my warning, Mr. Eyre," he stated without preamble.

"*Your* warning?" I was thinking of the anonymous message. "But surely——"

"My advice," he said irritably.

Oh yes. When I dined with him. About the dangers of associating with Harriet Leeson. I pretended not to know what he meant. He shore through my resistance like a razor.

"You know well what I'm talking about."

"But Father——"

"I am not your Father. I have no responsibility for *you*.

But I am responsible to weed out evil practices from my parish."

The angry, condemning look in his eyes roused my own anger. "You mean it's your duty to listen to tittle-tattle and slander?"

"Don't try my patience too hard, young man."

"What on earth are you talking about?"

"You know perfectly well." His spittle sprayed my face as he said, "Your association with Mrs. Leeson is causing scandal.

"I'm sorry to hear that. Am I supposed to have committed adultery or merely to be contemplating it?"

Father Bresnihan forced himself under severe restraint. I could see the hairy backs of his hands shaking as he gripped my car door.

"Don't fence with me, young man. You're impertinent." His face lost its tension gradually. The beautiful voice took on a note of appeal. "Dominic. You don't mind if I call you Dominic? Will you swear to me you haven't"—the pale face flushed—"you've no carnal knowledge of—no intention of——"

"Father, if you believe I have designs on Mrs. Leeson, you should warn her husband against me. Shouldn't you?"

He was silent a little. Suddenly I hated myself for these paltry evasions, and realised too how coarse I was becoming. *Nostalgie de la boue.* Harriet had been bringing out of me a brute I'd never realised was there. Yet even to think like this was a betrayal of her. I felt doubly ashamed.

"It is not so easy," Father Bresnihan muttered. "You three going about together, going to the bar over there. Do you realise, but for that the people would have drummed you out of the town weeks ago? Do you realise, they think of you as under his protection?"

It was certainly a novel thought to me, and a disconcert-

ing one. "But surely *you* aren't afraid of Flurry? Why
don't you talk to him?"

"Maybe I am. But I'm much more afraid *for* him. For
his soul. And yours, Dominic."

I liked and respected the man so much. I felt a curious
need to comfort him. But all I could say was, "I'm just
thinking how utterly inconceivable this conversation would
be in an English village street."

He smiled, but faintly. At that moment Kevin Leeson
hurried out of his store. "There's an urgent message for
you, Father. Come to my telephone."

As I drove off, two lines of verse slid into my mind—

> *There's a witness, an eye,*
> *Nor will charms blind that eye . . .*

If the Garda did make any investigation, nothing came of it.
For a week or so, things went on very much as before. In
the evenings, I was often at the Colooney bar with Harriet
and Flurry. I don't know whether Father Bresnihan had
exaggerated in the heat of the moment, but I was certainly
not aware of any hostility on the part of the Charlottestown
people. It was an unpalatable thing to think of the man I
was cuckolding as my protector: but by this time any sense
of decency, any compunction I might have had, were swept
away by my passion for Harriet. To the Charlottestown
folk, Flurry—I began to see it—was a kind of mascot: a
reminder of the great days, with the renown of his past
deeds still thick about him. I could only look upon him as a
ruin, a mouldering folly on some estate, its reason for existence gone. I could not dislike him, for he had the brash,
hearty charm of many Irishmen, but I could not take him
seriously. I remember once, when Harriet and I were rag-
ging about in the drawing-room at Lissawn, Flurry encour-
aging me to put her across my knee and give her a good

welting—how it struck me that we were like two mice play-ing with impunity in front of an old, paralysed grey cat.

I do not expect this sort of thing to commend itself to the reader. I am trying to tell the truth about this extraordinary relationship, so far as I can get at it across the long stretch of time. It had become clear to me by now that this ashen-faced, lumbering man was either impotent or largely ex-hausted by his wife's demands. And this led me into a deep-seated contempt for him—the contempt of a young animal for an old one which has lost its power. I had never tried to get to know him any better: what was there to know in this empty husk? And that, as it turned out, was a great mistake.

Harriet and I became more and more unguarded in our behaviour. I remember thinking—it is the nastiest point of my confession—that in our outrageousness lay our safety: Flurry could not possibly suspect us when we were so open in front of him—when we played so innocently before his eyes.

She herself did have certain compunctions. Though Flurry was away from time to time, only once did Harriet let me make love to her in Lissawn House. Flurry was in Dublin that night, and Harry a bit drunk. It was raining lightly: we could not go out to our usual place. She took me up to their bedroom—it was the first time I had seen it. That is the night of which I have the most vivid picture: the picture of Harriet standing naked by the window—the hour-glass figure shining in the moonlight, the groove of her spine, the dark, dark red gleam of her hair; and the river talking in its sleep below.

Oh, that was a famous night. How many times we made love, I daren't think. " Hurt me! " she kept crying. I drove my fingers into her body, punched it, pulled her head back by the hair over the side of the bed. She bit me viciously like a fox. She exulted in it all. When we were both ex-hausted, she whispered, " I feel like a cat that's had a saucer of cream "; and then, " I'll be black and blue to-morrow. I bruise so easily." I remembered that, as I walked back to the cottage at dawn, in a daze and feeling as if the marrow had been drained out of my bones.

Those bruises she showed me at our first picnic. She said Flurry had been knocking her about. But perhaps they were love-bruises. Flurry's. *Flurry's?* Some other man's then. So Harry was a liar. All right, Harry's a liar: what do I care? . . .

One evening at the end of June, having some shopping to do in Charlottestown, I looked in at Kevin's house to give him a cheque for my rent. Maire Leeson received me, told me her husband would soon be back, apologised—too profusely —for looking so dishevelled: she'd just finished baking. She took me into the chilly drawing-room, pressed me to have tea or a glass of sherry. I chose the latter. She bustled out, returning with a decanter of what proved to be the same sherry as I had drunk with Father Bresnihan. She asked me how my book was getting on. In fact it had recently got stuck: in the turmoil of my affair with Harriet, my characters had become more and more unreal, uncompulsive.

I told Maire the novel was not going so well. She asked a number of intelligent questions, and I found myself liking her and enjoying the discussion. I became aware how much I'd been unconsciously missing this kind of civilised talk the last two months: Harriet and Flurry never mentioned literature, and never evinced the slightest interest in my own books. Nor was Maire nearly so straitlaced as I had supposed. We got on to *Emma Bovary*, for instance, and she talked about it first from a literary not a moral point of view. But then she began comparing the situation of Emma in the provincial France of her day with that of a hypothetical equivalent in provincial Ireland now. Was she trying out the ground? Was I being manipulated?

After several glasses of sherry, I felt the qualms of a mild summer diarrhoea I'd been suffering from. I asked Maire if I could go to the lavatory (I almost put up my hand, so schoolmistressy did she appear.) Maire blushed, led me through Kevin's study to a door leading out of it, said she must go up and put the younger children to bed. Would I come back to the drawing-room? Kevin was expected any moment.

I had only just sat down when I heard the study door open. Two people entered. I heard Kevin's voice and one I did not recognise. It was slightly embarrassing, the idea of emerging from the loo into a business conference. Kevin and the other man, just audible through the thin deal door, were talking mostly in Irish, but now and then they broke into English.

"Force is no good at all," the other man said. "You'd be wasting your time. You should contact——" and then a name I could not catch.

I pulled the plug. When I went out into the study, only Kevin was there. I apologised for the intrusion: Maire had shown me into his lavatory.

"I certainly didn't mean to overhear——"

Kevin looked at me in a measuring way. "Overhear?" He had suddenly grown rather formidable.

"——your business discussion. Anyway, no harm's done. I don't understand Irish."

"You don't?" he asked neutrally. "Of course you don't. Why should you?"

When I'm nervous, I tend to babble. "I quite agree about the use of force, though. I'm against it."

"Are you now?" Kevin's curiously opaque expression changed. "Well, no harm done at all, as you say. C'mon in and have another drink. Maire'll look after you till I come back. I just have to pop out and see a fella for a minute or two. You'll have supper with us. No, I'll take no denying."

He led me back to the drawing-room. Maire had put the children to bed and was writing a letter.

" Give Mr. Eyre a drink, dear. I'll be back in two shakes. Then we can have supper, and maybe a song or two."

It turned out, after my little contretemps, a very pleasant evening. Kevin had a useful baritone voice, and I sang a few songs myself, ending up with " Oft in the stilly night." I made rather a hash of this; the whiskey Kevin had plied me with made it difficult to phrase properly that deceptively simple, long-breathed song.

There was something very endearing about Irish hospitality, I thought as I drove back, a little muzzy, to the cottage: spontaneous, take-us-as-you-find-us, yet with an agreeable touch of the ceremonious too—a sense of breaking bread with friends.

I left the car on the patch of grass beside the cottage. I flung open the door and entered. There was a disturbance in the air behind me. The next instant I felt a dreadful blow. My head seemed to burst open, then everything disintegrated.

Chapter 6

I became aware of an intense pain, as if a creature inside my head was trying to batter its way out. I tried to put up my hands and contain it or let it out: but my hands would not move. Somewhere in the background there was another pulsing noise, its beat desynchronised with the beating in my head.

To move my head caused me agony as if jagged lightning struck through it, so for some time I stayed quite still. I must have a monstrous hangover. But then, assembling my mind piece by piece I put together its last experience—the evening at Kevin Leeson's, the return to my cottage, the blow.

How long all this took, I do not know. But at last I got my eyes open and with difficulty focused them on the nearest object. It was leather. I was slumped on the back seat of a car, which presently proved to be my own car. A wave of nausea engulfed me, and I wanted to vomit. This made me aware that my mouth was stopped—by some kind of gag. I recollected cases of people suffocating in their own vomit, and kept still again, trying to control my heaving stomach.

After a while it was better. My eyes began exploring again, out to the steering wheel, the instrument board, the windscreen, and then beyond it. Like a baby, I had to compose the sense-data of my world into a coherent picture.

Sand, rocks, waves, a sky lightening with dawn. The picture seemed familiar. It was. Piecing it all laboriously together, I discovered that I was on the back seat of my car, and the car was stationary on the strand where Harriet and

81

I had had our first picnic. The day was breaking, the de-synchronised pulsing I had heard in my head was the sound of waves thumping on the strand. My hands were tied behind my back.

For a time I sat, content to know myself alive. Someone had clobbered me the night before, put me in my car and driven me out here. Why? Why this elaborate set-up? If murder had been intended, surely there were more effectual methods than dumping me on a strand where, lonely though it was, someone would sooner or later see the car and investigate? My assailant could not have thought his blow had killed me, or he would not have taken the trouble to gag me and tie my hands.

A warning, then? The third warning to "lay off it"? I felt again the disagreeable lurch of the heart which comes from realising that one is a target for some anonymous hostility.

It took a little time, in my muzzy condition, before I discovered that this slight lurching movement was not subjective at all. The car itself was moving, now and then, settling down little by little into the sand. Each time the relationship between its windscreen and the line of breakers beyond was subtly altered. And now I realised that the car had been dumped in that shallow concavity on the strand which I had been warned against. If it is quicksand, I thought stupidly, it's very slow quicksand.

But soon I noticed that the sea-line had come appreciably nearer. The tide was making. In half an hour, perhaps, it would pour into the depression. This might, for all I knew, stimulate the sluggish quicksand into greater activity. Or the sea might enter the car—yes, the window beside me was half open—and drown me without waiting for help from the treacherous sand.

"The cruel, crawling, hungry foam." I watched the line of breakers, hypnotised.

What goes on in one's mind when one watches the visible, ineluctable approach of death? I remember nothing but a suffocating panic. In stories, the prospective victim always finds some sharp edge on which he can saw through the rope that binds his hands behind him. I threshed about on the back seat, out of my mind with terror, but no sharp edge presented itself in the well-padded interior. I fought to loosen the grip of the rope on my hands, but there was no give in it. I managed to crawl over the front seat (the car had only two doors) and get my fingers on the handles; both doors were locked. I tried to chew through the plaster which clamped my mouth shut. Hopeless. I levered myself back on to the rear-seat. All I could do was to scream silently inside myself.

The car lurched and settled again. The sea was moving in faster to the kill—only fifty yards away now. It lay between me and the little grassy cliff out there where Harriet and I had first kissed. My mouth was sore; tears were rolling down my cheeks.

Desperately I fought myself—to accept what was coming, to die like a human being, not like a trapped beast: to die—not with dignity, that would be impossible—but at least with a little courage. I ought to make my peace with God, whatever that might mean. But I had no courage left, and composure was beyond me. All I could manage was a kind of fatalism, which quietened me a little as I watched the approaching waves.

So intensely were my eyes riveted to them that I did not at first take in the voice which was hailing me.

"Is there anyone there?"

I looked to my left. A black figure was running clumsily across the strand. When he got nearer, I saw it was Father Bresnihan. I leant my head towards the half-open window, nodding frantically at him. He came to the edge of the depression, recognised me, made a reassuring gesture, then moved towards me across the innocent face of the sand. I could see his feet sinking in at each step, but he got through to the car. Its running board must have been level with the sand now. He stood on it, tried the door, then leant in at the back and wound the window full open.

"It's all right, Dominic. I'll have you out in a minute."

Somehow he got his hands under my arms and with a tremendous effort of hoisting and pulling, dragged me out through the window. His strength was amazing. I fell flat on my face at his feet.

"Get up!" he cried urgently. "Can you walk?"

I discovered I could. My legs had not been tied. Supported by the Father, I dragged my way through the yielding sand on to firmer ground. There, taking a sizeable penknife from his pocket he sawed through the rope which bound my hands.

"Your wrists'll hurt a bit," he said, chafing them hard to restore the circulation. Then, with a decisive movement, he tore the plaster from off my mouth. I tried to mumble my thanks.

"Not a word. By the mercy of God, I saw you in time. C'mon, the strand'll soon be covered. My car's at the bottom of the lane. Can you walk that far?"

"Someone hit me on the head last night, and——"

"That can wait. C'mon now." Father Bresnihan pocketed his penknife, and carrying the severed rope, helped me to the landward edge of the strand. We forded the river there, and got into the car. He drove off straight away. On the way back to Charlottestown, he told me that he'd been up all night in a cottage on the hillside, comforting the widow of the man whose funeral cortège I had seen: she was now mortally ill herself.

I tried again to express my thanks. Extreme peril, if one survives it, makes one babble. Father Bresnihan cut me short. "It was providential, as you say." He looked at me sidelong. "I hope you'll profit by it. Providence may not give you another chance, Dominic." Well, he had every right to moralise. "I'll stop at Sean's garage to see if he can do anything about your car. A team of horses might drag it out yet, after the tide's gone down. That bit isn't the true quicksand, or you'd not be here now."

I thought the Father might improve the hour by reference to spiritual quicksands, but he forbore.

He put me to bed in his own house. After the doctor had examined my head, and told me I would live, I sank into a deep sleep. I must have slept round the clock; the next thing I knew was Kathleen, the housekeeper, waking me with a breakfast tray. "It's a soft day, Mr. Eyre. I hope you're feeling better now. The Father says will you get up by midday if you're able for it. The Garda Siocthana'd like to be having a word with you. . . ."

A soft day it was, but only climatically. When I walked into the little garden at the back to try out my legs—they appeared to be in working order—I felt the fine Irish rain, which always seems to have been poured through holes, infinitesimal in diameter, of the rose of a celestial watering can; threads of rain, all but invisible, which alight on one's face with the touch of spider-web filaments.

I came in soon. A pot of coffee awaited me in the study. I had not finished my cup when Father Bresnihan entered, a man in a suit of green thorn-proof tweed behind him, and made the introductions. It was my first meeting with Superintendent Concannon. He had a square-ish head, a pale and rather ascetic face (he might well have been an intellectual, a Maynooth-bred priest or professor, I thought), and a manner almost deferential.

After a few civilities, he told me they'd managed to get my car hauled out of the sand yesterday. It had been thoroughly examined, and Sean was now at work on it, to try and make it serviceable again.

"I take it you found no fingerprints."

"There's quite a few, on the parts the sea didn't cover. You had a narrow escape, Mr. Eyre."

I noticed Concannon's habit of tilting his voice up at the end of a sentence, giving to a statement the effect of a half-concealed question.

"You've had trouble before, the Father tells me. Did you inform the police?"

"Yes. After the last episode, I had a talk with the sergeant here. He doesn't seem to have got anywhere though."

"Casey? Ah, he's an eejut," said Concannon disloyally, smiling at Father Bresnihan and myself. It struck me that openness and informality must be very different from English police methods: nor, for the matter of that, would an English detective have allowed the local vicar to sit in on an investigation.

"Well now, we must hear all about it. Are you quite sure you feel able for some questions, Mr. Eyre? Good. I'll just get Cathal in to write it all down. If you'll allow me, Father?"

Concannon called through the door. A uniformed man came in, sat down and produced a note-book. I was led through the previous episodes—the search of my cottage and the shot from behind the bushes—Concannon helping me along with an occasional question. "There was nothing stolen? . . . Was there anything in your papers a fella'd be hunting for? . . . How long between the shot and your getting back to Lissawn House?"

When we came to the events of two nights ago, Concannon made me describe in great detail what had preceded them. I told him about going to Kevin Leeson's house, the contretemps in the lavatory and what I had overheard there, the pleasant evening which followed.

"How long was Mr. Leeson out of the house after he'd shown you back into the drawing-room?"

"Five minutes about. Perhaps a little longer."

"And what time did you leave?"

"Quarter to twelve."

"You're sure of that?"

"Yes. I looked at my watch and was surprised to find how late it was."

"Then you drove straight back to your cottage. You didn't stop on the way?"

"No. Straight back."

"Did any other vehicle pass you?"

"No. I've thought about this. It was physically impossible for Kevin to have arrived at the cottage before me."

Concannon gave me a curious look. "Why should he want to harm you?"

"Why should anyone?"

"But Mr. Leeson could have made arrangements with someone else during those five minutes or so he was out? Is that what's in your mind?"

"He *could* have, no doubt. But why on earth should he be gunning after me?"

"'Gunning'?"

"A figure of speech," I snapped irritably.

"I'm aware of the metaphor," Concannon replied with a touch of ice. "And you can't think of any other reason why someone should be gunning after you?"

"No."

Father Bresnihan, who had been sitting quite silent, studying his fingers, looked up. "That is not true, Dominic."

It was a very awkward moment. I knew it would be likely to arrive sooner or later, but I'd hoped it would somehow have been postponed. There was nothing to be done now but plunge in boldly at the deep end.

"Father Bresnihan thinks," I said, not looking at him, "that I've been paying too much attention to Mrs. Flurry Leeson."

The point of the shorthand-writer's pencil broke. A faint blush appeared on Concannon's face. The Father nodded at me approvingly.

"And have you, Mr. Eyre?" asked Concannon mildly.

"I like her very much, and I've been seeing her pretty often. Living nearby. She and her husband have both been very kind to me."

"I see. And you think your intentions have been mis-interpreted," said Concannon silkily, his voice tilting up at the end.

"The Father seems to think so."

Father Bresnihan's mouth twitched angrily, but he made no comment.

"Are you suggesting, then, that Mr. Flurry Leeson is behind these attacks upon you?"

"Certainly not. I think it's wildly improbable."

"A jealous husband?" Concannon let his voice trail away.

What could I answer? that Flurry was a complaisant cuckold?

"He has never shown me any signs of that," I said. "But no doubt you'll be finding out where he—and Kevin and everyone else were—two nights ago."

"I've already taken statements from them, Mr. Eyre." Concannon leant back, lacing his arms behind his head. "Have you a passport, Mr. Eyre?" he asked negligently.

"Yes. But not here. You don't need one for Ireland."

"I suppose, as a writer, you travel a good deal. Local colour—that class of thing."

"I've been to France. And Italy. And once to Greece. But——"

"Nowhere else in Europe? Germany?"

"Good lord no! Not with that Nazi gang in control."

"A godless lot of sinners they are," said Concannon. "You wouldn't object to sending for your passport and letting me see it."

"Of course not. But what on earth has this to do with——?"

"You'll do that, then. I'm most grateful to you, Mr. Eyre. And now we'll have to think how we can best protect you. Won't we, Father?" Concannon added cosily.

"Protect? You think it might happen again?"

"It might so. Have you a gun?"

"No. I didn't come over here expecting to get involved in shooting matches."

"Sure you didn't." Concannon's intelligent face broke into a purely boyish grin. "We'd best have the Father give one of his hell-fire sermons next Sunday, warning his flock against the sin of murder."

Father Bresnihan appeared to take this quite seriously. For myself, the word "warning" threw a fantastic idea into my mind. The Father's arrival in the nick of time to rescue me from the car—had it not been suspiciously pat? Perhaps he had organised the whole thing, not to kill me, but as a last warning. It was a bit strange that it should happen on the night he was sitting with the sick widow in her cottage on the hill. Of course, he would have needed an accomplice to stun me and drive me to the strand. But he was a man of absolute authority among his people; and his fanatical zeal against sexual irregularity was well established.

Hardly had this passed through my mind when I saw its grotesque absurdity. I must be suffering a delayed reaction from the knock on my head.

"So you're going back to your cottage?" asked Concannon.

"Yes. I'll bolt the door at night. If I remember to."

It was bravado, of course. Like many timid people, I sometimes had the urge to provoke the crisis which I felt lying
in wait for me, to get the thing over with. Concannon gave
me an undeserved look of admiration.

"Very well then. We'll be keeping your cottage under
surveillance for a while, till I get to the bottom of that
assault on you." He gazed at me reassuringly. "You're not
a very curious man, Mr. Eyre, are you?"

"How do you mean?"

"Aren't you interested in the statements I took from your
neighbours?"

"I thought that was the sort of thing the police kept
under their hat."

"Oh, we have *secretive* policemen over here. As well as
secret police. But I'm not the one nor the other."

Concannon now told me that, according to their statements, Flurry and Harriet were in bed when the assault took
place, Kevin and his wife were going to bed. Seamus
O'Donovan had said he was asleep, but he slept alone in a
room above one of the Lissawn outbuildings, so there was
no one to corroborate his evidence. The man of the cottage
a hundred yards down the road from mine said he'd been
woken by a car passing along the road about midnight, and
before he went to sleep again had heard a car passing in the
opposite direction.

"And now I want you to make me a list of all the other
people you've met since you came to Charlottestown. And
you'll write at once for your passport. But there's another
thing; the most important. If you'll be good enough to help
me with this."

"Yes?"

"I want you to think back over all the conversations
you've had since you came to Charlottestown——" Concannon was looking at me with a most serious, urgent expression—"and tell me of any occasion when you felt the

person you were talking to seemed specially inquisitive about yourself."

"That'd apply to pretty well everyone I've met."

"Ah, we're a nosy lot. Aren't we, Father? What I have in mind, Mr. Eyre—it's hard to define—but any man or woman who seemed to think, or maybe you gave the impression unwittingly, that you're not the man you give yourself out to be—a writer holidaying over here. Someone you felt was pumping you, to draw out your real identity."

"A nice metaphor," I replied. "But I really can't——"

"Take your time, Mr. Eyre. There's no hurry. It might have been in a shop, in the street, a chance encounter you thought nothing of at the time. In the Colooney bar. Anywhere. You have it now?" he added with a touch of excitement.

A bell had rung loudly in my mind. Colooney bar. I have an excellent verbal memory: so I was able to tell Concannon, almost word for word, that bit of my conversation with the Colooney manager the first night I was here.

"Haggerty asked if I was in business or government service. I answered, 'A sort of business. A one-man business.' I didn't want it put about just then that I'm a writer: and I was a bit irked by his inquisitiveness. Then he asked if I kept a shop. And I replied, just to mystify him, 'a very closed shop.' A curious expression came over Haggerty's face——"

"Describe it."

I tried to do so.

"And then?"

"The Leesons—Flurry and his wife—came in, and the conversation ended."

"The man you overheard talking with Kevin in the study —could that have been Haggerty?"

"Definitely not. Quite a different voice."

"Did you have any talk with Haggerty since?"

"Oh, quite often. But only the time of the day, gossip, that sort of thing, in the bar."

Concannon glanced at the Father. "So *that's* it! He's a simple-minded fella, Haggerty, isn't he?"

"He is," said Father Bresnihan. "But he likes to think he's crafty."

"Exactly."

"What *is* all this?" I exclaimed irritably.

Concannon smiled at me. "Don't you see the impression your words would have on a fella like Haggerty?"

"No, I don't."

"What you let slip in front of him—what he *thinks* you let slip—was that you're some class of spy: a British spy."

"Good God!" My mind raced like a propeller out of water.

"There was a lot of West Britishers—if you'll forgive the expression, Mr. Eyre—in the Dublin Castle intelligence service in the bad old days."

"But——"

"And the British'd want to find out just what's going on over here now, wouldn't they?—what's the feeling about neutrality? whether some of the extremists wouldn't welcome a German intervention?"

"Sure they'd never do that," protested the Father.

"But they'd use any opportunity to push the Taoiseach into getting back the Six Counties. And a war between Germany and England would be their moment. Naturally, the British'd want to know the strength of that feeling."

I was bewildered still.

"You see, Dominic, if the English Government thought we were going in against the North, with or without German encouragement, it would give them an excuse to invade us first. It's the Treaty Ports they'd be after."

"I see your point, Father. So it's not my alleged immoral

life, but my espionage activities, which have made me your parishioners' target," I said nastily.

"It would account for your cottage being searched," said Concannon. "But not necessarily for the other episodes. Did you ever visit Galway Bay or Clifden, with your great big field-glasses?"

"I often go into Galway. And I drove up to Clifden once. With my great big field-glasses. What an innocent bird-watcher has to put up with! But they're not Treaty Ports, are they?"

"They could be used. By smaller vessels."

"I think the whole thing's absolutely mad," I said with exasperation. "Confound your politics! It's all so—so amateurish."

"Dominic, there's no one so amateurish over here as an amateur politician. And no one so professional as a professional one."

"You have it, Father." Concannon gazed at me broodingly. "Michael Collins now—he had a short way with Castle spies. Maybe you ought to take the first aeroplane back to England." That upward tilt again at the end of the sentence.

I suddenly had a strong intuition—or was it a delusion?—that this calm, intelligent policeman was reserving judgment about me, that he had not convinced himself I was *not* a spy. It was an unpleasant sensation. Never before had I felt so completely a stranger in the land of my birth.

I decided I'd go into the attack. "If I *am* a spy—and I see you're not sure about it yet—duty would obviously require me to stick it out here. If I'm not, commonsense should tell me to go home at once. Well, I'm staying. Yet I'm not a spy. I'm just an Anglo-Irishman—beg your pardon, West Britisher—who doesn't like being pushed around. The Garda are welcome to investigate me: but also they're in duty bound to ensure that I'm not murdered."

A damnably pompous speech, but at least it had the effect of disconcerting Concannon.

"We know our duty, thank you, Mr. Eyre," he said stiffly. "I would like to take your fingerprints now, so we can eliminate them from the others on your car."

"By all means. But haven't your criminals over here learnt yet about the use of gloves?"

"We're a backward nation, Mr. Eyre." He smiled forgivingly.

Father Bresnihan had the last word. "There are criminals and criminals, Dominic. Like there are sinners and sinners."

Chapter 7

The next day I returned to the cottage. Sean had miraculously got my car running again. The front door was not locked; the key was in the drawer where I'd always kept it, my MSS on the table. I had a sense of anticlimax, ruffled by an occasional wave of fear. Would there be another attack? What form would it take? Concannon had told me he was putting a plain-clothes man in the cottage up the road, and indeed for a week or so I was to come across a man—or rather, a succession of men—desultorily filling in the potholes or trimming the roadside grass. And I heard footfalls at night, patrolling round the cottage from time to time. No doubt these were not local men: they would have been sent from Galway or Ennis. But, in a district like ours, everyone would know in a few hours they were not roadmenders.

That first afternoon I walked over the fields to Lissawn House. Flurry and Harry were in the kitchen, drinking tea. Flurry clapped me on the shoulders.

"Dominic! How *are* you! This is a great moment, a solemn moment. The returning hero. They ought to make a fillum of your hairbreadth escape. We must drink to it, Harry."

He lumbered out to fetch the whiskey. Harriet threw herself into my arms. "Are you all right? Did you get my message?"

"No, love."

"That damned priest! I bet he destroyed the note. No, it's all right. It was quite pure—just a message of sympathy from Flurry and myself." She looked up anxiously into my eyes, felt the back of my head. "My God, what a bruise! Are you really——?"

"G'wan, Harry. Give him a kiss. He deserves it," came the voice of Flurry from the door.

"I was just feeling this lump on his head. It's a whopper."

"I bruise easily."

She gave me a smile of complicity. "All right, I will. I've fallen for the wounded hero." And she kissed me quickly, full on the lips, in front of Flurry. I was embarrassed; yet her recklessness was flooding into me again like a tide.

We talked a while. I had to relate the whole story to them. Harriet's eyes were sparkling. "At last something has happened in this dead-alive hole!"

"Thanks very much, Harry. I just hope somebody else'll provide your entertainment next time."

"Next time?"

"D'you think your local assassin won't have another shot at bumping me off?"

"Boo, you're not windy?"

"Of course I am. What do you think, Flurry?"

The pale grey eyes in the ashen face glanced at me uneasily. Was it the look of a would-be murderer who had failed? Or that of a lazy man who didn't want to be involved in trouble?

"I don't know at all at all. I had a word with Seamus, but he s heard nothing about who the fella might be. Has Concannon any ideas about the—the—what the hell's the word?—the motive?"

I told him the theory that I'd been taken for a British spy. The notion excited Harry's childish mind. Flurry was unimpressed and said, "*You* a spy! God help us, what'll they think up next?" I was obscurely annoyed by this. It was not the first time Flurry had made it clear that, in his mind, I was no man of action.

"You'd better come and live up here for a bit. Seamus and I—you can hire us as bodyguards."

"Thank you. But I wouldn't think of giving you the trouble."

"Now he's in a huff. You don't really fancy yourself at the cloak-and-dagger stuff, do you, Dominic?"

That damned Irish intuition again. A slob like Flurry had no right to it.

"Ah well," he continued remorselessly. "If you're determined to set up as a lone wolf, at least you'd better keep your door locked. Keeping the wolf inside the door. That's a good one, Harry."

"Ha, ha, ha," I mirthlessly replied. "You know it's interesting about the key. How did the man who lay in wait for me inside my cottage the other night *know* that the door would be unlocked?"

"Nobody locks his door here."

"Not even at night? Not even when he's suspected of being a British spy? The point is, they couldn't *bank* on the door being unlocked. So they'd have a key, just in case. Who would have a duplicate key? The lock was changed when your brother did up the cottage."

Flurry gave his boisterous bellow of laughter. "Sure that's great! Isn't it killing, Harry? So the Mayor it was who bumped you. It's a lovely idea. But Kevin's a coward. He'd no more——"

"Kevin couldn't have done it himself. He could have had it done, though."

Flurry had a sobered look. "But why in mercy's name?"

"If he's secretly engaged in some extremist activity, and *if* he thought I'd discovered something about it—accidentally or as a spy for the English——"

"Ah, get on!"

I told them about overhearing Kevin and the stranger talking in the study. "He couldn't be certain I don't understand Irish. And I must say it is rather strange that he at once invited me to dinner, kept me under his eye the whole evening, and the moment I got back to the cottage——"

"So you'd never have had time to pass on the information to anyone else?" Flurry's lack-lustre eyes had lit up now: I could see the old flying-column commandant look through them. His next action was characteristic. He hurried from the room, and I heard him bawling outside for Seamus.

While he was gone, I asked Harriet about the night I'd been set on. "Flurry was asleep with you, wasn't he, by midnight?"

"Yes. Why? Are you jealous?"

"For God's sake! Be serious for once! You'd have woken up if he'd left you?"

"I should think so. We did go to bed a bit sozzled, though," she replied indifferently. "What's all this in aid of?"

"I just wanted to make sure Flurry hadn't crept out and clobbered me himself."

Harriet laughed merrily. "Oh boy, what drama!"

"Of course he couldn't have driven me to the strand and left me there in the car. He'd have had to walk all the way back."

"I expect he had an accomplice," she said with childish mockery. "Oh Dominic darling, you *are* an ass! Be your age!"

At that moment Flurry returned with Seamus O'Donovan. Seamus congratulated me on recovering so well from what he called, rather oddly, "your accident."

"Never mind about that. He's alive. Dominic, tell Seamus what you just told us."

I did so.

"Now then, Seamus me boy, you're the eyes and ears of

Charlottestown. Did you ever hear tell of my brother's being mixed up in I.R.A. extremist activity?"

Seamus took his time. The brilliant blue eyes were gazing away towards the mountains far beyond the window. " I did not," he replied at last.

" No rumours at all?"

Seamus shook his head. " Not about him. There's always gossip of this political stir or that. Some of the Civil War irregulars is always trying to stir up trouble. Sure there's some ones round here is scared of their own shadows. But I never heard a one putting the talk on Kevin."

" The fella Mr. Eyre heard with Kevin—was there any stranger in Charlottestown that day?"

" There was. A fella came to Sean's garage for petrol. He seemed in a hurry, Sean told me—could hardly pass the time of day with him."

" What time of day would he have passed?" I asked.

" About half six, Sean said."

" That could have been the man I heard talking to Kevin, then?"

" Did Sean describe him?"

" He did not, Flurry. I'll ask him to. I'll ask around and see if anyone else saw him."

" You do that, Seamus. But you'd only come at the half of it," said Flurry. " There had to be one fella taking Dominic to the strand, and another fella with a second car to get the first one away."

" There would so. Unless Mr. Eyre's attacker dumped him there and just walked back to wherever he lives."

They argued it for some while. I felt more and more like a dummy which had been used for an operation. Now these two ex-gunmen had taken it over. Courteously excluded from the conversation, I simmered with impatience at their maddening Irish blend of openness on the surface and opacity beneath. A devious race.

Flurry and Seamus were still at it when I decided to leave. Absently they bade me good-bye. Harriet walked a little way along the river with me. When we were out of sight of the house, she pushed me against a tree and rammed her body at mine. I kissed her close, but could not respond more. Father Bresnihan's words were in my mind; and I had a backlash of compunction about Flurry.

"Don't you want me any more, darling?"

"Of course I do. But my head—I'm not absolutely fit yet."

She looked at me with that pitiless female insight. Why does one need lie-detectors when there are women about? However, she only smiled. "Will you be fit two nights from now? I'll come to you by the river, if it's a fine night. Do you know, it's more than a week since last time?" She bit my ear hard, then whispered into it, "I'm wild for you, my poor little wounded hero. You'd better come or there'll be trouble. Look after yourself till then."

And she was off through the trees, humming to herself, not looking back . . .

So all went on as before. Well, perhaps not quite as before. There was a touch of desperation now in our love-making; and with it a certain tenderness seemed to have entered Harriet's attitude towards me, which I had not felt before. She could never be a clinging woman, but the way she sometimes gazed at me now—there was a new softness, an almost sacrificial look.

As for myself, I was still riding high in the insolence of lust. Now and then I spoke to Harriet harshly, testing my power over her. I did not seek to plumb the depth of her feeling for me. I had written to Phyllis, saying I did not think she and I were suited: Harriet had never asked me to do so, nor did I tell her I had. Phyllis wrote back without rancour, releasing me. But it never occurred to me that I might marry Harriet. She was a priestess in the temple of the body, adept and still a little mysterious: one did not marry priestesses. Beside, such was her sexual arrogance that I always felt in her an antagonist, a challenger. It was this arrogance which kept bringing my infatuation to white heat again, and prevented her (so I believed) from even noticing that in most other ways I found her the reverse of stimulating.

Love-affairs have their watershed—a point where, unobserved may be by the participants, they level out and will soon start to go downhill. Ours, I should think, was reached that July. Disenchantment had not yet set in: but, as I say, there was a touch of desperation—like that one gets from blazing autumn flowers when the first frosts of the year have come.

The result of this desperation, heightened by the coming war and my own equivocal position in Charlottestown, was to throw Harriet and myself together more constantly, and to make me still more reckless where Flurry was concerned. There had been no more attacks, no more warnings, no anonymous letters. It was as if the place had washed its hands of me. Father Bresnihan was distant, but polite. I saw the Kevin Leesons several times during the fortnight after the episode of the strand: they both seemed solicitous about my health and my work, and I could perceive no trace of guilt or anxiety in Kevin's manner. Concannon came to see me twice, but he was distrait, and uncommunicative about his investigations: I imagined these had reached a dead end. My passport he found to be in order: I had not visited Germany, on this one, at any rate: but, if I were a secret agent, no doubt I'd have had a drift of false passports at my disposal.

What form Flurry's and Seamus's investigations were taking I had no idea. I assumed that Flurry was making them, not for my sake, but for his brother's. Though he talked about Kevin as a figure of fun, Flurry had, I came to realise, a certain protective feeling for him: also, as Harry told me one day, it would be a disastrous thing for Kevin to be disgraced, since he helped Flurry out with his debts from time to time.

From Flurry himself, so boisterous, so boring, I'd begun to develop a sense of immunity. He was like a stationary obstacle—a bunker on a golf-course, say—which one had learnt to avoid, and then got a kick from skirting ever more closely. Harriet and I did indeed seem to lead a charmed life. One day, for instance, we were making love in the hay-loft. We heard Flurry come in below. "Are you there, Harry?" he said. And she called back, "I'm up here. With Dominic. What d'you want?" "What the hell are you doing?" he called good-humouredly. "We're up to no good," she replied, not even reaching for her jumper. "Ah, go on with you!" She bit me hard on the shoulder, strad-dling over me. "Shut up! He may——." I tried to push her off. "Don't be so windy!" she whispered. "He won't climb ladders." Flurry's footsteps receded, out into the cobbled yard. "You see? it's quite safe. Now I'm mounted. Come on."

It must have been a week later—the last week in July—that I drove them to a small town in Galway. There was to be a horse-show there, and a few races in the afternoon.

"Harry's to ride a horse we sold last year to a fella out there," Flurry told me. "I'm putting my shirt on it. Even Harry couldn't lose with Barmbrack under her."

We set off at eleven o'clock, Seamus at the back of the car with Flurry, Harriet beside me, heavily made up, in her best riding clothes.

"Where's your cap, Mrs. Leeson?" asked Seamus when we had gone a few miles.

"I don't need it, not for a flat race."

"Cleopatra wants to show off all that beautiful hair," remarked Flurry. "You ought to have a cap, you silly cow."

"Oh, pipe down." She gripped my thigh painfully. I never ceased being surprised at the strength of her delicate hands. She was already in a state of high excitement.

"I don't know if you're a devotee of the turf, Dominic," said Flurry, "but you'll find our races out here in the West very different from Ascot."

"He will," said Seamus.

"No top hats or champagne. Just horses and riders and most of them couldn't sit a spavined ass."

"Sure your wife could ride a whirlwind," said Seamus. "But watch out now for the last furlong, Mrs. Leeson. There's apt to be a drove of drunks on the rails there, and you'd never know what they might be doing. Barmbrack's a nervous animal, remember."

The steep main street of the town was jammed when we arrived. Countrymen in thick black suits, tinkers, beggars, hordes of children, priests, Gardai; cars and traps and ass-carts; a few county-looking women; a sprinkling of tourists, some of them wearing Connemara jerseys and sweating in the heat. A gentle babble came up from the crowd. The air smelt of whiskey, porter, Guinness, petrol and dung.

We followed a belated horse-box down the hill, and parked in a field near the river. A lane led to the grassy expanse where the show was being held. It was lined with cheapjacks bawling their wares, sinister-looking characters inviting the concourse to try their luck at Spot-the-Lady and other money-losers, and stalls of lemonade, repulsive-looking food and souvenirs. Through the pandemonium cut a megaphone voice, adjuring the laggards in some class to "put a sthreak into it! Numbers 3, 7 and 16, we're waiting for you. Come on now, bring those horses in! We can't wait all day for you."

We took our sandwiches and drink to a low ridge that overlooked the arena. Harriet toyed with her food, then went off at her rolling gait to find the owner of the horse she was going to ride.

The results of a class were given through the loudspeaker. "It's a fix!" exclaimed Seamus. "It's a bloody fix! The owner of that horse bought a couple others last month from the chief judge. Sure he'd give her the prize if she showed a tinker's caravan beast with the mange. He'd give her the prize if she was riding a three-legged stool. Is there no decency left in this bloody place?"

An altercation broke out with a group of men who dissented from Seamus's opinion. So I slipped down to take a closer look at the judging ring. I have nothing against horses: they are preferable, *en masse,* to writers—better looking and debarred from speech. In Ireland too, the horsey folk are more animated than their English counterparts.

A class for Connemara ponies was next to be judged. The glossy, wild-eyed creatures were led round the ring, stepping daintily, elegant as porcelain figurines. A group of Germans, the women looking like film stars, the men with dark glasses, huge binoculars and expensive tweed suits, were talking nearby in loud, authoritative voices. I moved away, to come across Kevin and Maire Leeson. We exchanged a few words. Then I said, nodding towards the Teutonic group,

"I don't know how you can stand those people in your country."

"They bring in money," replied Kevin. "Beggars can't be choosers."

"You brought Harry over, did you?" asked Maire, in neutral tones. "Do you go racing much in England?" She faintly accented the last word.

"Harry, and Flurry and Seamus. They're all here some-where. Flurry says he's put his shirt on Barmbrack."

"He'll not have any shirts left if he goes on this way."

"You think it'll not win after all?"

She shrugged. "I'd be in terror of putting my money on any horse. Betting's a vice with some, like alcohol."

"One little bet, and you might become an addict?"

"My father nigh went bankrupt that way, God rest his soul."

While we were talking, I noticed a nondescript man make a slight sign to Kevin, who presently sauntered off after him through the crowd.

By four o'clock the judging was over. I found Flurry—who, like most of the men on the field had paid periodic visits to the town's snugs—and we strolled with Seamus to the race track. The finish was at the lower end of the field: the course stretched away a mile along the grassy flat by the river. By now Harry must have ridden out there to the start—I'd not set eyes on her all the afternoon and was feeling a bit disgruntled.

We found places by the rails on the far side from the river. Seamus was going on about another "fix." Apparently Barmbrack's only dangerous rival, a horse called Letterfrack, was now to be ridden, not by his owner, but by a quite well-known English amateur rider who was staying as his house guest. The bookies had shortened the odds against Letterfrack.

A bell clanged somewhere, and relative silence fell. Harry's was to be the last race on the programme. We watched three others, Flurry getting more nervous all the time. I did not like to ask him how much money he actually had on Barmbrack. Certain characters, on the rails opposite us, were growing unruly. A Garda stood behind them, but they paid him no attention.

"They're off!"

This was Harry's race. Standing on tiptoe I trained my field-glasses on the distant horses. Out of the blur, two presently detached themselves—a powerful roan, ridden by a man in full hunting kit, and Barmbrack, a black horse. Harry's hair was streaming, like a flag in a gale. As far as I could tell, she was a few yards behind Letterfrack, but going well. The finish was twenty yards to our left. The two of them were now fifty yards away from us, the roan still in the lead. "Mother of God! I can't stand it," Flurry muttered.

"Bring her up now!" yelled Seamus.

As if she had heard him, Harry leant forward, spoke into the horse's ear, and dug in her heels. Barmbrack shot forward.

And then it happened. A drunk on the far side of the rails gave a shout and took a swipe with his ashplant. No doubt he intended to put off the English rider. But his reactions were slow. At this very instant Harry, close to the rails, was squeezing past the Englishman. Whether the drunk actually hit her horse, I could not tell: but, alarmed by his shout and the flail of the ashplant, the nervous Barmbrack swerved to her left and cannoned violently into Letterfrack. I saw Harry flung to the ground. The Englishman just managed to keep his seat and rode on to the finish.

Seamus turned to Flurry and me, tears in his eyes. "And she had it won."

But Flurry had vaulted the rail and was running towards his wife, who lay motionless on the turf. Seamus followed. They ignored the other horses galloping down on them. I saw Flurry go on his knees beside Harry, stare wildly at her, lift her head on to his lap. Whatever he was saying to her could not be heard in the pandemonium. Many of the crowd were convinced that the Englishman had bored into Harry and unseated her: a threatening group of men followed him towards the paddock; a line of Gardai formed up against them.

As I came up, Flurry cocked his head towards the far rails and said to Seamus, " Mark that fella and keep him for me." Seamus withdrew. Flurry looked up at me: tears were rolling down his cheeks. " Here you are at last, Dominic."

" Is she——?"

" Concussion. Where the hell are those fellas with the stretcher?"

Harriet was lying on the grass, her hair fanned out: with all that make-up on her face, she looked like a doll some child has flung on the floor. A crowd stood around us in a respectful circle; voices commiserated with Flurry. He glanced up wildly. " Letterfrack's near hind must have struck her as she fell." He bent down again. " Harry, old girl, wake up."

But she did not. She was still unconscious when we got her to the hospital. A doctor told us presently that she had no bones broken, only severe concussion: " She'll be as right as rain in a day or two, Mr. Leeson."

" Please God she will." Flurry mopped his brow. " She's a head like iron. Mind you look after her well," he said to a nun standing beside the doctor: then, to the latter, " I've a little business in the town. I'll be back in an hour. C'mon, Dominic."

We walked back into the main street. I had felt excluded since Harriet's fall. I could not show more than a friend's proper concern. And now, as we threaded through the crowds, I had the helpless sensation of an object drawn into a field of force.

" And fifty pounds gone down the drain too," Flurry muttered. He turned into a pub, but after one look round went out again, myself at his heels.

" Who're you looking for?"

" A fella I have business with."

Several people hailed Flurry, but he paid them no attention. Which was as odd as him going into a pub and not taking a drink. In the third one we visited, I spotted Seamus at a table with a glass of Guinness before him. He nodded to Flurry, then rose unhurriedly and tapped the shoulder of a man at the bar.

"You're wanted, mister."

The man turned round, a hulking red-faced fellow.

"Who wants me?"

Flurry stepped forward. "I do."

The man reached for his stick, but Seamus had quietly removed it.

"You're the bloody fella who lost my wife the race."

"Ah, c'mon now. Sure I was only aiming a stroke at that Englishman."

"Well, now you'll have a stroke aimed at you—you son of a clappy whore."

Several of the man's friends grouped round him, threatening Flurry with words and gestures. Instantly Seamus was in front of them, hand in coat pocket.

"If anny of you lousers interfere I'll plug him in the belly," he said, his voice as deadly calm as Flurry's. The group shrank back a little.

"Will you fight then," said Flurry, in a voice so cold it would have taken the skin off your hand. Once again, in this shambling, drifting man, I saw the commander of the flying column who had over-matched the Black-and-Tans in ruthless savagery. "Will you fight? or will I put a rope round your neck and drag you home to your poxy mother's sty?"

Enraged, the man lashed out. Flurry blocked the blow and countered with a swing that nearly sent him over the counter. The man snatched a pint glass from it, smashed it on the counter's edge and thrust it at Flurry's face.

"Drop that or I'll plug you," shouted Seamus.

"Let him be," Flurry commanded. "Keep out of it,

boy." He backed a step, then let fly with his boot at the man's knee. In jumping back from it, the man got off balance: before he could recover, Flurry brought the side of his hand down on the man's wrist and the tumbler fell to the floor.

"Now he'll have him destroyed," Seamus said to me happily.

Flurry's opponent had sobered up and he was a powerful fellow. But Flurry began to demolish him. He took a few round-arm swings himself to the side of the head; and then his huge fist shot out, with an impact that must have broken the man's nose. As he covered up, head in hands, Flurry hit him low in the belly. The man bent double, retching in agony, which enabled Flurry to lock his neck under one arm and drive the other fist into the man's face—four times in a couple of seconds. He then flung the fellow reeling to the floor, and before he could roll away stamped the heel of his boot down on to the man's crutch.

What Flurry would have done next to his victim, I hardly dare contemplate. But Seamus dragged him away from the writhing, screaming hulk on the floor.

"That's enough, Flurry! Stop now or you might hurt the bugger."

Flurry looked round the bar, panting. "Anyone else like a work-out?" The offer was declined. Those who had not jumped over the bar counter were standing stiff against the far wall. "All right then, Seamus. March."

He led the way out of the pub. As we walked back up the street, I said to Seamus, "Lucky you had that gun."

"Gun? What'd I be doing with a gun? I borrowed this out of your car." Seamus pulled a spanner from his pocket and handed it to me with a slight flourish.

"I need a drink," said Flurry.

"You're out of condition," Seamus told him. "If that fella'd persevered, he'd have stretched ya."

" Well," said I, " he'll not rob you of fifty pounds again."

" Wha's that?"

I repeated the words. I shall never to the end of my days forget the look Flurry gave me then—a look of amazement, which turned slowly into the most naked, shattering contempt.

Chapter 8

Three days later, Flurry and I fetched Harriet from hospital. She seemed quite well again. There had been no repercussions from Flurry's brutal assault on the man who had lost her the race—in Ireland, I could well imagine, private quarrels would be kept private: to go to the police would stamp a man as an informer.

The afternoon of her return, Harriet walked over to my cottage. She asked me to tell her all about the fight, and listened with sparkling eyes as I did so. No woman, I suppose, dislikes being fought over; but I found her reactions rather crude.

"I'd never have thought Flurry had it in him. Not now."

"Well, he beats you—so you used to tell me."

She lowered her eyes. After a moment's silence, she asked, "Are you windy? Afraid he might do the same to you?"

"He'd have a right."

"But he likes *you*. He's not a jealous man, give him his due."

"How do you know? Have you talked to him much about me?"

"He never talks to me much."

"Oh, come off it! Stop being evasive."

"We don't have intimate conversations any more," she said stubbornly.

I knew we were on the edge of a quarrel. Ridiculously, I felt myself on Flurry's side, wanting to pierce through her indifference. "But for God's sake, don't you have any feelings for him at all?"

"That's good, coming from you!"

"I'm asking you, Harriet. You may not be highly articulate, but he's your husband——"

"Don't be so bloody rude." She got up to go, but I pushed her back into the chair.

"Does he or doesn't he know that we are lovers? Surely the point is of some interest to you?"

"I don't know. And I couldn't care less."

A thought struck me. "Why do you suppose he used such violence on that chap in the pub?"

"Because he'd lost him a lot of money, I suppose."

"That's what I thought. Now I wonder. I believe he's been boiling up with resentment about you and me, and he took it out on that fellow."

"What an absurd idea! You *would* think up something intellectual like that."

"It's not intellectual, you dumb cluck. You say he likes me. Possibly he 'likes' you too. Therefore he restrains himself from beating up your pretty boy. Therefore he unleashes himself on someone else."

"Oh, balls!"

"How complaisant do you think a husband can get? Do you imagine he'd just sit back and accept it if—if you and I ran away together?"

That was a mistake. Her face changed. "Would you run away with me?" she said seriously. "That *would* be romantic. We could——"

"Oh Harriet, do come out of your woman's-magazine fantasies. You know I couldn't marry you." And, having said it, I knew it was beyond any question true.

"Why not? Don't you love me any more?"

"It's not a matter of being in love," I replied uncomfortably. "You'd soon get bored with me—like you did with Flurry. We're not—not suited for each other."

"So you're tired of me already."

"Marriage doesn't all take place in bed."

"You mean your intellectual friends would despise me."

"Oh, damn my intellectual friends! In a year, we'd have nothing to talk about. What interests have we in common? You won't even talk about Flurry."

There was a long silence. At last she said, "So you've stopped wanting me."

"No, love. Indeed I haven't."

"Come here then." . . .

So she had her triumph. My body was still in thrall to her. Whistle and I'll come to you, my lass. Afterwards, I could rebel against my servitude—against the idea of being dragged down to Harriet's own level (this time it had been the cottage floor, where we mauled each other like wild animals). But my rebellion was tempered by the tenderness which, for me, was still an aftermath of each lovemaking. Every time, the naked sex-object became, when we lay back exhausted, this particular woman—vulnerable, unaccountable, but my dear accomplice—an accomplice all the more intriguing because I never absolutely trusted her.

A few days later, the three of us met in the Coloney bar. I happened to mention that I was going into Ennis the next day. Harriet, who had seemed rather preoccupied, soon asked me to drive her home. She told Flurry she had a headache, and we left him soaking in the bar.

Half-way back to Lissawn, Harriet asked me to stop the car. I assumed she wanted to make love on the back seat— we had done it often enough before. But she said, "Will you buy me something in Ennis, darling?"

"Yes. What'd you like? A gold necklace?"

"I need some quinine."

"*Quinine?*"

"Yes. It must be quinine powder."

"But why?"

"I don't want to buy it here."

"What d'you want quinine powder *for*, my love?"

"If you must know, I'm going to have a baby," she answered flatly.

My first, unworthy reaction was—the old trick. Then I grew ashamed of myself. I was filled with remorse, and fright.

"Are you sure? How long have you——?"

"Two months."

"You should have told me, darling. We were mad, not to use——"

"Well, you've done it now," she said good-humouredly. "But one Dominic is quite enough for me."

Was she lying about the whole thing? Suddenly, I did not care. A gush of tenderness spread over me: I felt absurdly protective.

"But isn't it dangerous?"

"Oh, it's worked before."

"Quinine powder?"

"Yes."

"With whose baby?" I asked suspiciously. "I thought Flurry——"

"Never you mind. Just get me some. I thought falling off that horse'd have done it."

"And if it doesn't work this time?"

"I'd have to pretend it's Flurry's. A miracle. Like what's-her-name in the Bible."

That took my breath away. To father this putative child on Flurry! Yet I also felt an ignominious relief.

"You couldn't do that!"

"I've done it."

"What do you mean 'done it'?"

"Must I spell it out? I gave Flurry an occasion to think he might have begotten a child. A month ago."

" But I thought——"

" He's still capable. Just."

I was staggered by all this. My picture of Harriet changed once again. If she'd really been set on running away with me, she'd have used her pregnancy as a lever on me, not made plans to deceive Flurry.

" Well, you seem to have everything worked out," I said ungraciously. " You might have told me sooner, though."

" If I had, you'd have run away. Without me. Wouldn't you? It'd have given you a lovely excuse."

" I shall still have to go home before long," I replied, nettled by the accusation in her voice.

" Sufficient unto the day. I'll have had another month or two with you, anyway." Harriet said it so sadly, so honestly, it nearly reduced me to tears. Her mood changed again. " Well, at least you could say it, even if you don't mean it."

" Say what, darling?"

" Wouldn't you *like* to have a baby by me?"

Here she is again, I thought—once repulsed, and infiltrating back.

" I—I hadn't thought about it."

Her face turned to me, mysterious in the darkness. " Well, you'd better go to bed and think about it now. Go on! Start the car, or Flurry'll be here on his motor bike." Her voice blurred into sobs. " God knows why I ever fell in love with you." . . .

I bought Harriet what she needed. Two days later, Flurry sent down a message by Seamus: Harry was poorly and wanted me to come and cheer her up. I put aside my book —it had been moving slower these last weeks and now had reached a block: my characters seemed unreal to me, dwindled like a fire in the hearth when strong sunlight pours in on it.

Flurry took me up to their bedroom. She lay in the big bed, pale and childlike without her make-up.

"What's wrong?" I asked.

"Oh, just a tummy upset," she replied, grinning at me.

"The silly fool won't see a doctor. Feel her skin, how hot she is."

I put the back of my hand against her cheek. It was burning.

"My head's making ringing noises," she complained.

"Well, Dominic, I'll leave you to persuade her to call in the doctor. She's so bloody obstinate, she won't be told by me."

When he had left us alone, I said, "Has it worked?"

"Not yet. I took three times the dose you're allowed," she added with her gamine smile. "Flurry's in a great state. He thinks I'm dying."

"Does he know?"

"Don't be a bloody fool. He'd kill me if he thought I was trying to get rid of a baby he'd believe was his own. Don't look so gloomy, darling. I want to be amused."

I told Harriet a dream I'd had last night. I was a fly caught in a web. All round the edge of the web was a cordon of spiders, whose faces turned into the faces of my neighbours—Flurry, Seamus, Father Bresnihan, Kevin, Maire. They began advancing towards me. I struggled to get away, but it was like walking through a quicksand. Suddenly I was myself, alone on that fatal strand, and the waves were creeping towards me.

"And then I came and rescued you?"

"Then I woke up."

"Wasn't I in the dream at all?" she asked with a touch of pettishness.

"You can't be everywhere, love."

Harriet stroked my hand. "You *could* give me a kiss. I'm not infectious."

It was like kissing a child good night.

"I'm worried about you. Are you sure that stuff isn't dangerous—such a big dose?"

"I lived last time." After a pause, she said, "Don't you want to know who it was last time?"

"If you want to tell me. Not Flurry?"

"It was Kevin."

"Good lord! *Him?*" I thought she must be light-headed. Or was she pulling my leg?

"Yes. I seduced him. Like I seduced you," she said gaily. "Only it didn't take me so long. Don't frown, darling. I gave him up when you came along."

"Not till then?"

"I expect I could get him back when you go home," said Harriet, with her sublime sexual arrogance.

"I expect you could," I said dully.

"You're not jealous?"

"Aren't I? I daresay he's more jealous, though."

"Oh, he doesn't know about us."

"I should think everyone in Charlottestown knows about us. Suspects anyway. Jealousy feeds just as well on suspicion as on fact."

"Aren't you pompous!" . . .

And the quinine powder did not work. Harriet seemed undistressed: her craving was unabated. It was August, and a break in the weather prevented us making love out of doors. She would come to my cottage, slinking over the pastures like a vixen. Each time, I said to myself feebly, "That must be the last time." Yet I was prevaricating. I knew I ought to leave at the end of the month—why break it off till then?

The mountains kept their heads hidden in shawls of mist. I felt claustrophobia in my little cottage, with the vast, empty countryside weighing on it all round.

My book was at a standstill: one day I drove into Galway to find reading-matter, having exhausted the meagre facilities of local bookshops. I also borrowed books from Maire Leeson, who was welcoming but preoccupied: Superintendent Concannon had been on at them, she threw out, "asking eejut questions." I found myself making excuses to go into Charlottestown—shopping, a chat with Sean at the garage—simply to meet other human beings. Perhaps I was not made for the solitary life after all. I also found that I was going into the Colooney bar at times when I was pretty sure Flurry and Harry would not be there. Haggerty had become a little more distant, if no less deferential: I seemed to be a fixed object now in his landscape.

Harriet's visits to the cottage were the only other breaks in my boredom. Short breaks, too, for once we had made love there was little to say. I was bored by her chatter about trivialities, the coarseness of her sensibility: this made me feel like a traitor: I tried to conceal it, but less and less could I respond to her except physically. The old magic was gone, and I was left with the expense of spirit in a waste of shame. Yet I felt a responsibility for her, and could not steel my heart against the essential pathos of her life.

I was in this doldrum state of mind, counting the days like a schoolboy before I would go home, almost wishing that something would happen—some new melodramatic attack upon me, even—to break the monotony and bring me alive again, when one night I heard a tapping on the door. My heart gave a lurch: but I forced myself to the window. There was just light enough through it from my oil lamp to identify the figure of Father Bresnihan outside. I unlocked the door and let him in.

"The weather's clearing. We'll have a fine day tomorrow."

I set him down with a glass of whiskey, feeling I had an ordeal before me.

"You'll be going home soon, Dominic?"

"At the end of the month, I expect."

He asked me about my mother, my life in London, my new novel.

"It's got hopelessly stuck. I doubt now if I could ever write here—anywhere in Ireland."

His intelligent eyes were fixed on mine. "Too much drama outside, the inner drama is crowded out?"

"I dare say you're right."

The Father deliberated for a few moments. "I'm sorry I spoke to you intemperately that day in Charlottestown. You are not of our persuasion, after all."

"I think you had every right."

"It's very kind of you to say so. It encourages me to ask two questions I know are impertinent."

"Ask away."

"You're not planning to—people you've met over here, friendships you've formed—you wouldn't be collecting material for fiction?"

"Most certainly not, Father. Of course, one never knows what experience of one's own may not find its way into a book one day. But it'd have suffered a sea-change. I can promise you, I should never want to traduce you, or betray any confidence——"

"You misunderstand me." A slight frown had knitted his brow. "To put it bluntly, I can imagine nothing so—so despicable as making up to a young woman for the sake of getting material for a——"

"Nor can I," I replied indignantly. "I'm not that sort of exploiter."

Father Bresnihan lit another cigarette, his hands shaking. "No, I'd never have believed that of you."

"And you've asked your second question before—am I living in sin with Harriet Leeson?"

His eyes held mine. "Well, are you?"

Why I decided to fence with him no longer, I shall never know. I was tired of fencing. And he was a good man.

"Yes, Father."

He drew in his breath sharply. But his beautiful voice was almost apologetic as he said, "Oh, Dominic, have you no sense of sin? Can't you realise what mortal danger you've put her soul in?"

"Father, how can you realise what love between man and woman is like?"

"Love? You call an animal coupling 'love'?" He visibly restrained himself. "Do you intend to take her back to England and ruin her husband's life? He's not much else left, you know."

"No. I shall say good-bye to her at the end of the month."

"I see." He looked up at me piercingly. "Why do you wait till then? Because it suits your convenience?"

"That's a bit harsh."

"And don't you deserve it? Now listen to me, Dominic. Every time—you and Mrs. Leeson—" his mouth twisted with disgust—" you are making it more difficult for yourself —the addiction becomes heavier. You may not believe in mortal sin. But you're doing yourself damage that may be irreparable. You know as well as I do that you and Mrs. Leeson have nothing in common. To use her only in the way of the flesh is cynical—a cynicism that leads to despair —and it leads to an unconscious contempt for all women. Once you have founded your relationship with but one woman on lust alone, you diminish the whole area of a future marriage: you may wish to be whole-hearted for the wife you choose, but your heart will be warped." He sighed. "I know you have been grievously tempted. If your own father were alive, I'm sure he would tell you to put yourself beyond the reach of this temptation now, not to stay open to it for weeks more."

I felt the force of his words; yet they seemed somehow beside the point—and an over-simplification of the whole matter. I nearly told him about the baby (but was there a baby coming? would it be mine?). I stood in some awe of Father Bresnihan now.

He smiled gently. "You're a bit of a moral coward, Dominic. Like us all. You should tell Mrs. Leeson to her face, next time you see her, that it must stop. You must be ruthless, not only in resisting her entreaties, but in beating down your own sexual pride."

I began to speak, but he over-rode me. "And I must beat down my own cowardice. I've put off talking to Flurry Leeson. I shall go to him to-morrow night, and tell him he must keep his wife in order."

"But——"

"Does he know about her relationship with you?"

"Honestly, I'm not sure. He knows we're friends, of course. He's never even hinted anything else to me."

"I see." The ascetic face was quiet in the lamplight. "Either he is condoning mortal sin, or he's a very much stupider man than I believe him. It's all right, Dominic; I won't betray your confidence. I'll just tell him plainly that his wife is a cause of scandal in my parish, and I can tolerate it no longer." The old note of authority came back into his voice.

"You'll be taking a risk, Father."

"Flurry's a man of violence—has been. But I do not think he'd raise his hand against a priest. What are your own feelings about him?"

"Oh well, I like him, up to a point. But he does seem to lead a pretty futile life. I suppose I look down on him a bit. He's friendly, hospitable—it's just that he's not my sort," I said uncomfortably.

"No more than his wife is. It's soothed your conscience to think him a worthless fellow who doesn't deserve an attractive wife, doesn't respect her, doesn't pay her any attention?"

"I'm afraid that is true."

"Oh, Dominic, have you once tried to put yourself in his place?" The thrilling voice deepened in earnestness. "A soldier whose occupation is gone? A man who drinks to forget that? A human being with nothing left him but a down-at-heel demesne and a flighty wife? Have you no pity for him?"

I found myself inexpressibly moved by Father Bresnihan's words. Long after he left that night they were echoing in my mind. . . .

The next morning was glorious summer again. I met Harriet at midday, exercising a horse in the demesne. I told her I wanted to have a talk with her.

"Come to our place on the river. Ten o'clock. Father Bresnihan rung to tell Flurry he'll be visiting him then. I'll slip out."

She put heels to the horse before I could say another word. My next ordeal was going to be even more difficult than I'd thought.

When I arrived that night on the spit of grass by the Lissawn, Harriet was already there. She sat up in her white night-dress, and I soon realised she was more than a bit tipsy. The river was still running fast after the rains, but the air was warm.

"Harriet, I must talk to you."

"Love me first. I want you."

"No."

"Do what you're told, my darling." She stripped off the night-dress and stretched herself before me.

"No, Harriet, we've got to stop."

"But why?"

"It's not fair on Flurry."

She sat up abruptly, her body glimmering in the faint light. "What on earth's come over you, Dominic? *He* doesn't mind."

"How do you know?"

"Why've you suddenly started to fuss about Flurry? Don't you want me any more?"

I tried to explain, without bringing Father Bresnihan into it, why we should go on no longer. It was futile.

"If you've suddenly gone pi, you must take me away and marry me. I'd go anywhere with you."

"We've had all that before, love. You know we're not suited to live together. You'd be bored with me in a few months."

"You mean you'd be bored with me. Why can't you be honest and admit you're tired of me?"

"It's not that at all." The smell of her skin came to me in a waft of the night-breeze. There was a long silence.

"So you're going to run away and leave me with your child. That's a lovely brave thing to do, I must say."

"How do I know it's my child?" I was stung by the contempt in her voice. "How do I know you're going to have one at all?"

Harriet gasped, as if I had struck her. Then she turned an angry face to me. "My God, you are a heel. Whose d'you think it is? Kevin's? Well, he's more of a man than you."

"I don't care whose the child is. All I'm saying is that I won't do this any more to Flurry."

"But you're quite happy to let him carry the can for you, aren't you? *Aren't* you?"

"No. I'm not happy about it at all."

"So you'll go and cough it all up to him? Your wife is pregnant by me, and I've just seen the light? What a hope!"

I kept silent.

"Somebody's put you up to this," she said suspiciously.

"I did have a talk with Father Bresnihan last night."

"I *knew* it! That bloody priest! What the hell's he poking his nose in for?" Her voice had turned to fury. "I could kill him—hypocritical busybody!"

"He's not like that at all."

We wrangled for almost an hour. Then Harriet said, "Oh, shut up! Come into me. Just once more. What does once more matter?"

Kneeling up beside me, she pushed her breasts into my face and began tearing at my fly-buttons. Her body was so hot, so beautiful. Yet I felt a momentary revulsion from it which helped my resolve to stand firm. We fought a while, then I threw off her hands and ran away through the trees. I could hear her sobbing behind me, then nothing.

But that night I could not sleep much. My mind kept churning over all we had said to each other—and all I should have said. I had done badly. I should have tried to explain more kindly my reasons why we must part.

And then all the love which had been between us came flooding back. It had *not* been just animal coupling: there had been affection and tenderness too. Scenes from our past played themselves over in my mind. I had deserted Harriet when most she needed me. I was a coward. She would never come back now. One cannot finish an unfinished thing by putting a brutal full-stop to it.

At dawn, some impulse drove me to dress and get up. I was empty with loss. She would never come back to me now. As if our place of assignation might give me some comfort, my steps were taking me back to that spot by the Lissawn river.

And Harriet was awaiting me there. I ran out from the trees, my heart leaping with joy, all my resolutions forgotten. Her night-dress still lay where she had cast it off. In the light of dawn, her prone body was pearl-white, her out-spread hair black as night. She must have gone to sleep when I had left her. I hurried to wake her and get her home before Flurry awoke. She must be terribly cold, lying there naked all night, the silly girl.

I shook Harriet by the shoulder and spoke to her. The shoulder was very cold indeed. Frantically I turned her body over. The front of it was a mad pattern of gashes, which looked like small black lips, and the blood they had oozed was nearly black too in the dawn's light.

One recovers much quicker from the first shock than is imagined. For a minute perhaps I was paralysed, gazing down at the spoiled body, feeling nothing. Then I thought "Never touch a murdered body, leave it to the police." Well, I had only touched the shoulder, to roll her over: there was not a speck of blood on my clothes. Why "murdered" though? Had my rejection made Harriet kill herself? Ridiculous. She'd not have brought a knife to her assignation last night, or stabbed herself all over if she had. And there was no knife anywhere near—I verified this in searching the thick grass to see if I had left any trace of my own presence.

My first impulse had been to run for help to Lissawn House. But now I knew I could not face Flurry, dare not explain why I'd come out here at dawn. And who would believe me? They would find out she was pregnant, find out that I had been her lover. Guilty lovers—it's a common-place—sometimes kill the woman they have made pregnant. The police would not look further than me.

I bent and touched Harriet's cold cheek. Her eyes stared up at me indifferently. I turned and walked away into the trees, furtively, as if I had indeed killed her.

PART TWO

Chapter 9

I stumbled back to the cottage, boiled myself tea and an egg, passed the time of day with Brigid when she turned up—all in a daze. And presently the wound began to hurt. I was responsible for Harriet's death. If I had not left her last night, it would never have happened. Was it some wandering man who had found her naked by the river, raped her and killed her? Or maybe Flurry himself, overwrought by his interview with Father Bresnihan, had made this maniacal attack upon her, his suspicions turned to certainty at last by the priest's words.

But then a dreadful thought struck me. I had been overwrought myself last night. Perhaps my personality had split. Perhaps, unremembered by me now, my alter-ego had returned to the river and stabbed the woman who had become an encumbrance to me. I climbed to my bedroom, frantically examined all my clothes. Not a trace of blood anywhere. I stripped—my cunning other self might have gone back naked to kill her. No blood-stains on me, no signs of a struggle. But I could have plunged into the Lissawn afterwards, and washed them away.

The idea that I might contain a maniac unmanned me altogether. I threw myself on the bed, sobbing, muttering " Harriet. Darling. Tell me I didn't do it. I'm sorry, love. Forgive me. For deserting you."

Presently, over the top of the fuchsia hedge, I saw two cars speeding towards Lissawn House. It must be the police. They'll break their springs at that rate.

I tried to collect myself for the next ordeal. I must tell them the truth—about everything except my meeting with

Harriet last night. That, I dare not do: it would put my head straight into the noose.

The knife, though! I went downstairs and feverishly examined the cutlery in the kitchen drawer. The knives were all clean; so was a penknife I kept on my writing table. So that's all right. But, if I'm a schizophrenic, I'd have washed the knife or thrown it into the river, and now have no recollection of doing so.

Schizophrenic? *Paranoiac?* Supposing Harriet's murder was the latest action in this extraordinary persecution campaign against me? The attempt to drown me on the strand had only just failed. My assignations with Harriet might have been spied on. And, after the last one, X could have killed her, knowing that the guilt would fall upon me. A subtle way to get rid of me.

I was appalled at myself for thinking only of my own predicament, while Harriet was lying cold by the river. No, they found her hours ago. That's what the police have come for.

I was sitting at my desk when Concannon arrived with the Charlottestown sergeant. His politeness had retreated to a great distance.

"Good morning, Mr. Eyre. May we come in? I have some questions to ask you."

"Please do."

(Don't say more than you need. Don't be gushing. Don't be unnatural.)

"Will you tell us your movements last night? From six p.m., say, to six this morning." His voice tilted up at the end.

"Well, I had dinner at the Colooney. Then I drove back here. After that there were no movements, except climbing up to bed."

The sergeant was writing busily.

"What time did you go to bed?"

" About ten-thirty."

" You had no visitors before that? You were alone here?"

(Time to show a little curiosity.) " Yes. Why? Was someone prowling around after me? I thought all that was over."

The eyes in Concannon's fair-haired, square head were almost dark-blue in the shadowy little room. Every time I looked up, they were fixed on mine.

" Did you have an assignation with Mrs. Leeson last night?"

" No. Not *last night*. (Clever.) Why? Does she say I did?" (Not so clever, perhaps.)

" You admit she is your mistress?"

" Yes. *Was* my mistress."

Concannon's eyes sparked. " Why do you say ' was '?"

" Because I've broken it off with her."

" When did you do that, Mr. Eyre?"

" Yesterday morning."

" She came to see you here?"

" No. It was in the demesne. She was exercising a horse. I said I must have a talk with her: I'd come to realise our association was wrong. She rode off and left me."

" What made you ' realise ' this, Mr. Eyre?"

" Father Bresnihan did. I had a long talk with him the night before last."

" Did you now? I see. You met Mrs. Leeson in the demesne. You told her then you wished to break it off?"

" No. I said I must have a serious talk with her. The breaking-off was still in my own mind only. But she *may* have suspected my intention. I'd told her several times that she and I were not suited for a permanent—for marriage."

" I see. And when do you propose to have this serious talk with her?"

" Well, I was rather funking it. (Careful.) She's not gone and done—anything silly?"

"Why do you ask that?"

(Impatience legitimate here.) "Well, for goodness' sake, Mr. Concannon! You'd hardly be asking me all these questions about her if all was well at Lissawn House."

He was evidently a little taken aback. (Now don't get over-confident.) There was a pause.

"Did Mrs. Leeson seem to you a suicidal type? Has she ever threatened——?"

"Good lord, no. She'd be the last person to—— You said, '*Did* she seem'?" My voice shook a little: this was not acting. "You'd better tell me, hadn't you?"

Concannon's eyes pierced into mine. "Harriet Leeson was found dead early this morning."

This must be a murderer's most difficult moment. How can any simulated reactions—shock, amazement, incredulity, horror—possibly ring true to a trained policeman? But the words "Harriet" and "dead" brought the live Harriet unbearably into my mind, put her deadness to me as if for the first time, so that my response was genuine.

"Oh, no!"

Concannon and the sergeant surveyed me in silence, as the wound of my grief broke open and I wept. After a while I pulled myself together.

"But she'd never kill herself. It's incredible."

"She did not. She'd been stabbed a number of times, on the breasts and stomach," said Concannon flatly. "Her body was lying by the river. A curious thing is that there was a lot of dried blood on the grass beneath her, yet she was lying on her back when Seamus found her. He says he did not turn the body over."

"On the grass? Not that grassy spit which runs out into the Lissawn? A hundred yards from the house?"

"That's the place."

"We—we often went there," I said, broken with true emotion.

"At night? You had no assignation to meet her there last night?"

I shook my head.

"You didn't make one, and then decide not to keep it?"

"No."

"Then what was she doing there, *stripped*, with a night-dress close by her?" asked Concannon in a pouncing way.

I shrugged my shoulders. The sergeant's ears were growing redder and redder.

"Did she strip for anyone but you?—and her husband of course?"

"I hope not. She did *tell* me that she'd had another lover here."

"And who would that be?"

"Kevin Leeson, she said."

"Glory be to God!" ejaculated the sergeant. "Asking your pardon, sir."

"But I never knew if she wasn't just trying to make me jealous," I added. "Tell me one thing. Did she suffer?"

"The blow that killed her pierced the heart. But there were others first, by the bleeding. There'll be an autopsy, of course."

(And then they'll find she was pregnant. The biggest nail in my coffin. Or will they?)

Concannon started the questioning again, calmly and ruthlessly, trying no doubt to trap me into contradictions, or just to fray my nerve. After another hour of it, he relaxed. "I've some men coming any minute. Have you any objection to them searching the cottage, Mr. Eyre?"

"None at all. I'm getting used to searches."

He gave me a wintry smile. "And you'll not be moving out of the district till our investigations are over."

"No. I only hope they won't take so long as your investigations into the attempt to murder *me*."

The sergeant's bovine face was brick-red. His Irish puritanism had been outraged by all this talk about sex and naked women.

"Will I clout him one, sir?" he suggested to Concannon.

"You will not."

When the two plain-clothes men from Galway arrived, they were certainly thorough. Under Concannon's eye they went through every article of clothing in the cottage, poked into every hole and corner: later, I noticed they were quartering the little patch of garden, turning over the rubbish dump, examining my car.

"Well?" I asked Concannon when at last they were finished.

"The results are negative, Mr. Eyre. I hope they'll continue so, as far as you're concerned. Can you tell me anything more now?"

"I've nothing more to tell you."

He gave me a strange look. "You know, if Mrs. Leeson had been expecting you last night, it'd account for a lot that puzzles me. Was she apt to walk out in her night-dress in the dark hours?"

"Only to meet me. So far as I know."

"Would you call her a promiscuous woman?"

"An experienced woman, certainly. But promiscuous? —— Oh, for God's sake, leave me *alone*," I burst out.

At the door, he turned. "Flurry Leeson is in a terrible bad way, Mr. Eyre."

He gazed at me austerely, like a Judgment angel, and went out to his car. . . .

It was not till the evening of the next day that Flurry sent for me. I found him sitting in the kitchen with Seamus. He looked a wreck, a charred derelict, his face more than ever the colour of dead ash.

"This is a dreadful thing, Flurry. I don't know how to——"

His lack-lustre eyes regarded me.

"All right, Seamus."

Seamus sent me an indecipherable look, then left the room.

"Give yourself a glass. You'd best pour another for me: my hand is shaky."

I did so.

"I can't believe it," he muttered. "I can't yet believe it." His eyes swivelled upward. "They're burying her on Friday. You'll company me?"

"Of course."

"You were a friend of hers. She set great store by you." He lifted a quavering hand. "Mind you, I'm not asking more. *I don't want to know anything more.* Y'understand me?"

I nodded dumbly.

"Maybe she *was* a bitch. That's my affair. I'll not have any damned priest coming here telling me I must control her. I loved that woman, Dominic. I loved her, y'understand. She could have gone to bed with my own brother, if it'd make her happy. So long as it brought the light into her eyes. We understood each other. Sure I know this place hadn't much to offer her. But I gave her everything I could. She was all I had."

Those were his words. I'll never forget them. On paper they look maudlin. But they filled me with an agonising contrition. That I should have thought Flurry had beaten up that man in the pub for losing him the bet! I should have realised, when I saw him rush on to the race-course and cradle her in his arms. Now he was teaching me the meaning of love. This shambling, provincial alcoholic had loved Harriet in a selfless way which put me to shame.

So I thought, abashed by the dignity behind his words,

utterly convinced by them. I wanted to blurt out a confession there and then. But how could I burden his sorrow, piling my own remorse on top of it?

"I'm just after hearing from Concannon. Harry was pregnant."

I stared at him, appalled.

"She'd told me—a month or two back—hinted she was that way. And I didn't believe her. I—it'd been so long, y'see. I never thought I was able for it," he mumbled, gazing into his whiskey, almost inaudible. "I laughed at her. *Laughed* at her!"

My mind was in utter confusion. So Harriet had already taken out her insurance policy; she'd deceived me when she said she could always put it on Flurry, *if* the worst came to the worst. Or was the child really Flurry's, and she using her pregnancy to blackmail me into marriage? I stared round the shabby kitchen. Already it had the makeshift look, like a transit camp's, of a place where men are living alone.

"It might have changed our life—a baby," Flurry resumed. "I'd always wanted one." His watery grey eyes suddenly turned to granite. "So now I've two lives to take revenge for."

"Revenge?"

"I'm telling you, Dominic. Whoever did this, *whoever* did it, I'll find him and I'll kill him. After that, I don't mind what happens to me."

"But——"

"What have I to live for now?"

A silence.

"It must be someone living nearby. Seamus says there wasn't a tinker within ten miles that night. There was no strangers in Charlottestown at all."

I remembered Flurry and the Tans, and shivered inwardly.

"I wish I could do something," I said vaguely; then took a plunge. "Concannon suspects me."

"You? Dear God, what'll the man be saying next?" Flurry gave a ghost of his wheezing laugh. "D'ye mean it? I believe you do."

"I suppose it's natural for him to——"

"But you were fond of Harry."

"I loved her."

It was out at last. I felt an overwhelming relief.

"Of course you did," said Flurry—but a little uneasily. I had to make it crystal clear.

"I mean, she'd—she'd been my mistress. I'm sorry."

His eyes swerved from mine. He seemed sunk again in stupor. I could hear the kitchen clock ticking through the long silence. At last he spoke.

"Now I don't want to talk about that. Didn't I tell you so?"

But I had a compulsion to go through with it now. I told Flurry the whole story of the night Harriet was killed— how Father Bresnihan had persuaded me I must put an end to the affair, how I had met Harriet by the river, and found her dead there the next morning. Flurry listened to me in silence.

"Was it you killed her?" he said at last. "Tell me the truth."

"It was not."

"You swear to it?"

"Yes. But ever since I've felt responsible. If I hadn't left her——"

"Never mind about that."

"I didn't dare tell Concannon I'd been out by the river that night."

"Well, I won't inform on you," said Flurry with the shadow of a smile.

The disagreeable thought flashed across my mind—if

Flurry had killed Harriet himself, I'd now put myself in his power: he had only to tell Concannon what I'd just confessed. Or, more likely, take the law into his own hands.

It was the moment of truth between Flurry and myself. He shook his great grey head like a tormented bull. I could not see him as the murderer of his wife. But he had an animal cunning and a history of violence.

"Father Bresnihan will tell you about the talk I had with him."

"No doubt he would. But he's just after going into retreat, Seamus tells me." Flurry looked at me unseeingly. "If he'd not gone blathering on that night, I'd maybe have walked out to find Harry before it—— But what with the drink and his homily, he had me finished. He'd hardly set out walking home before I was snoring in bed. I was still asleep at half six next morning when Seamus beat on my door. He'd just found her."

"He was out early."

"Seamus doesn't sleep well since the Trouble. He was very young then. Sometimes he gets up and wanders about the demesne, in the night or the dawn. Concannon chased him about it. He's searched through Seamus's clothes and things. But sure, he'd no more do such a thing than I would. Not Seamus."

In the fading light, the fuchsia and the bank of montbretia outside the window were turning monochrome.

"I'm glad you don't think I could have—you'd have every right to suspect me, Flurry."

"But you were fond of her."

The simplicity of it took my breath away. "Yet an Irish writer said that every man kills the thing he loves."

"Ah, that's all cod. Y' haven't the steel in you, Dominic. If you'd seen the wounds—but of course you did. No one strikes a woman like that, but in a rage of jealousy or a great passion of—— Ah no, I'm not an intellectual, but

I can see a fist when it's raised up before my nose. Sure you'd no reason to be jealous at all. And you're a man wouldn't lose control of his passions—they'd never be strong enough for you to have trouble mastering them."

Coming from Flurry, who had never before shown any tendency to character-analysis, these home truths were unpalatable. His next remark was even more disconcerting.

"Tell me now, when did you and Harry first take a fancy to each other?"

I stared at Flurry. This was beyond everything. With the intuitive tact I could never get used to in him, he showed me the way out of my embarrassment.

"I've a need to talk about her, Dominic, and there's nobody else I can talk to. She's dead, and we both were fond of her, so why shouldn't we talk about her? You'd be doing me a favour."

So the most bizarre part of that evening began. A cuckold and an adulterer exchanging reminiscences of the woman they had loved. I suppose the censorious would see it as morbidity in Flurry—a kind of mental voyeurism, but it never struck me like that. We had both consumed a lot by now, though Flurry said at one point that drink no longer had the power to make him drunk. I felt he wanted to possess himself of my share of Harriet. Between us, we recreated her, so that she almost seemed to be back in the room, reading one of her trashy magazines, a presence preternaturally vivid. I learnt much about the early days, when Flurry had just brought her over to Ireland. I told much about my feelings for her—even that I'd realised recently how incompatible we were.

Only later did it seem odd to me that her baby was never mentioned during these confidences. Surely Flurry must have had some suspicion that I might be its father? It was to worry me a great deal the next few days.

When at last I rose to go, Flurry took me by the arm.

" Why don't you come and stay here a while? Better than the two of us brooding in separate houses."

" Thank you, Flurry. But I couldn't do that."

" And why the hell couldn't you? I need you—you're a clever man—we could find the fella who did this, between the two of us."

I still refused him. Which turned out a mistake . . .

The next morning, Brigid failed to turn up. I drove into Charlottestown, to meet a strange reception. My good-mornings in the street were pointedly ignored. A group of children spat at me. In two of the shops and the post office I was received in silence: the post-mistress did bring herself to sell me a few stamps, but the shop-keepers paid no attention to my orders. At the garage, Sean said he had run out of petrol. I remonstrated with him, for I had just seen him fill up another car: he only walked into his garage, sullenly keeping his eyes from mine. In the Colooney bar, the deferential Haggerty gave me a look, between fright and defiance. " You're not drinking in this bar, Mr. Eyre. From now on."

" What the hell d'you mean? The law compels you——"

" Them's my orders. G'wan out with you now."

It was a boycott. I began to feel panicky. I walked along to Leeson's store, where I had always purchased the bulk of my provisions. I gave my order. The assistant said he had instructions to give me no more credit.

" But this is ridiculous. I've always paid my bill at the end of each month." I took out a few notes. " If you must have cash, here it is."

A pause. " I'll speak to the manager." No more.

" Well, speak to him."

" He's not in. What will you be wanting, Mrs. Rooney?"

" Then I shall speak to Mr. Leeson."

I went out in a rage. Two corner-boys spat at my feet.

"That's the fella's after murdering Mrs. Flurry," said one. "Yerrah, go drown yourself, mister." "Bloody Englishman," screeched the other. They rushed into the road, scooped up horse-dung and started flinging it at me. The street seemed to fill with people, staring at me, shaking their fists.

I pushed through them and rang the Kevin Leesons' bell. Then, throwing the door open, I went in. Maire appeared, looking harassed. "I'll be with you in a minute. Sit down now and rest yourself."

She was away five minutes. I had leisure to think of my predicament. If I left Charlottestown, the police would see it as the move of a guilty man, and pull me in: if I stayed, I should be starved out.

And who could have organised this boycott but Kevin Leeson himself?

Chapter 10

Maire came in, brushing aside a strand of auburn hair with the back of her hand. The children were out on a picnic, she said, in her most social manner: they'd be sorry to have missed me. I cut through her small talk.

"I've been boycotted in this town, Maire."

Her eyes started out at me. "Boycotted? What d'you mean?"

I told her the happenings of the last half-hour. She seemed genuinely startled. "But that's a terrible thing. Kevin must have a stop put to it. I'm afraid he's away to-night, but——".

"Kevin must have *started* it."

"Dear God, sure he'd never do a thing like that!"

"He owns the Coloney: they refused me a drink. He owns the store: they refused to sell me provisions. No one's going to do that here without Kevin's say-so."

"But—it's not possible. There must be some mistake. Dominic, why should he want you boycotted?"

I could have said "because I cut him out with Harriet Leeson, and he's in a rage of jealousy"; or "because he's up to some shady political manœuvre and thinks I'm a British spy and wants me out of the place." But, looking at Maire's distress, I couldn't bring myself to do it.

"The people here seem to think I killed Harriet. I hope Kevin didn't put it into their heads."

A certain wariness came over her face. "Now why on earth should he do that?"

I shrugged.

And suddenly her control snapped. "That wicked, wicked woman," she cried. "I know I shouldn't be saying it, but we're well rid of her. Everyone was happy here till she came." Maire rose abruptly from her chair, and rearranged some ornaments on the mantelshelf.

" 'Everyone'? What harm did she do you, for goodness' sake?"

"Agh, you all fell for her painted mouth and her saucy ways." Maire flung round at me, angry tears in her eyes. "She was no better than a harlot, that one!"

"Flurry loved her," I protested.

"She twisted him round her finger. Delilah and Samson. She was the ruin of him."

I let that pass. "It's not just him you were worried about."

Her eyes avoided mine. "I don't know what you mean."

"You were jealous of her and Kevin. Weren't you, Maire?"

She looked at me indignantly. Then, to my extreme embarrassment, she was on the floor beside my chair, gripping my knees, bursting out in a tempest of sobbing. I stroked her hair gently. In the dull misery I had felt since Harriet's death, I turned to Maire just because she was a woman, a mother figure. She must have repressed this jealousy so long, for she was a proud woman, that it broke out now like an elemental fury. I could feel the heat of her body raised by the flooding tears.

At last she pushed herself up and sat down again, mopping her eyes. She gave a little nervous laugh. "I don't know what you must think of me, making such a fool of myself."

"You've nothing to be ashamed of, Maire."

"I never thought I had it in me to be such a jealous woman. And I never had reason to be—not till *she* came along."

"But," I said awkwardly, "do you *know* that Kevin ——"

"She couldn't let men alone." Maire's eyes, brilliantly green again after the tears, stared at me. "Why was Kevin away so often at night? He got angry if I asked him. I never dared ask him if sometimes he was with Harriet. I expect she was shameless with him—the way I could never be." Maire blushed. "I can tell you things I wouldn't tell anyone else: because you're a stranger—well, not a close friend—a sophisticated man."

"Oh, I'm not that."

"I'm not—not a passionate person," she went on, blushing again. "I suppose she gave Kevin something I couldn't."

"Well, it's not the end of the world for you, is it?" I said gently.

"No," she replied in a small voice. "At least I gave Kevin children. Now, I'm forgetting my manners. Won't you take a glass of whiskey?"

We raised our glasses to each other. Maire took one of my cigarettes and smoked it inexpertly as a young school-girl. It was to prevent her bringing up my own relationship with Harriet that I said,

"What were all those idiotic questions you told me Concannon has been asking you?"

"Oh, it all started with him inquiring about our movements the night Harry—the night she died. Kevin got angry about it."

"Well, Concannon has to ask all of us about that. You were both at home, I imagine."

Maire looked at me strangely. She seemed to be trying to make up her mind about something. She took a deep gulp of whiskey, then came out with "He's terrible secretive—my husband, I mean. He hates people to be inquisitive about his comings and goings. Half the time he doesn't even tell me where he's off to."

"Yes?"

"He had a business appointment in Galway late that afternoon. He started back along the coast road, and about eight miles from here his car ran out of petrol. It's a lonely road—d'you know it?—and there was no petrol pumps open that time of night, so he walked home. He didn't get back here till near midnight. I was in a great taking."

I reflected that the road, about a mile from Charlottestown, passed quite near the Lissawn demesne.

"Concannon was on to him—just where he'd left the car? how long had it taken him to walk? did he meet anyone on the way? Eejut questions. Kevin had Sean drive him next morning early with a tin of petrol to where the car was. He'd parked it on the grass beside the road. Sean's given evidence about that."

"Why should Kevin get so angry then?"

"It was all the other questions upset him. Who was the fellow he met in Galway? Where? Why? He had the answers, of course. Another time Concannon came—it was only yesterday—he started pestering *me*. What state was Kevin in when he got back? Had he ever run out of petrol before? I said Kevin was tired and irritable when he got home, and went straight to bed. D'you know, we've had Concannon's men searching this house," she exclaimed indignantly. "It made me wild. I was hard set explaining it to the children."

Maire poured herself another whiskey absent-mindedly, then apologised and gave me one too. She was flushed. I perceived she was not used to drinking.

"You were worried by Kevin arriving so late?"

"*Worried?* Why, I even went out to——"

Maire clapped her hand to her mouth, in an absurd schoolgirlish gesture.

"Went out to look for him?" I prompted.

"Now I've given myself away, haven't I?" she replied,

too brightly. "It was all right. Katie sleeps in for the children."

She took another gulp of the whiskey. "It's desperate strong. Oh, I forgot to put any water in it. I'll be leading myself into bad ways."

"How far did you go, Maire?"

"How far? Oh, I see. I took my bicycle a mile or two along the road. I thought he'd be coming back that way, not the main road. I was in a great terror he'd had an accident."

"What time was this?"

"Half ten? Eleven? I don't remember exactly. He'd said he'd be home by nine, you see. Then I thought, well he may have taken the main road after all, and he'll find me out, so I bicycled back in a lather. I got home only a little before him."

"Did you tell Concannon this?"

"I did not. It's no business of his."

"But you told Kevin?"

"I did so. It made him wild."

"Why on earth should it?"

"He went on as if—as if I'd been spying on him that night."

The word "spying" pointed up a falsity I had vaguely felt in Maire's narration. Sipping my whiskey, while she went out to greet the children who had just returned from their picnic, I sought to define it. Something about her manner had not rung true: it was almost as if she were repeating a story she had got by heart.

Then light broke. Kevin had returned a little before midnight, Maire only a little before him! Therefore, on her bicycle, she should have caught him up on the road. She had left the house at 10.30 to 11. She would reach the end of the track to Lissawn in about ten minutes ("I bicycled a mile or two along the road "). What was she doing, then, for the best part of half an hour?

When Maire came back into the room, I said at once, "Perhaps you were."

"Were what? I don't understand."

"Spying on Kevin."

The green eyes flashed at me. She looked almost beautiful, with the colour on her high cheek-bones. Her mouth was trembling. Before she had time to speak, I went on, "Jealousy doesn't shock me, Maire dear. How long did you spend in the Lissawn demesne that night?"

For a moment I thought she was going to hit me. "How *dare* you? You must be out of your mind! I never set foot——"

I interrupted, pointing out the discrepancy of the times. "You see, Maire, either you were bound to overtake Kevin on the road, or else you bicycled along the track beside the Lissawn gates and went home that way."

She held out a bit longer, but I could not afford to relax: if she was in a trap, I was in a far worse one. "This is between us two, Maire. Please be honest with me."

Then at last it came out, incoherently, piece by piece. For some weeks before, she had noticed in her husband a nerviness, and a reticence unusual even for him. "He said once he thought there were men following him." The day he drove to Galway, Maire felt an uneasiness, a duplicity about him—and a kind of hangdog bravado, which always had aroused her suspicions about him and Harriet. She even felt something wrong about the naturalness of his references to the Galway trip and his affectionate leave-taking. "He seemed excited underneath, perhaps a little apprehensive."

Alone in the room after the children had gone to bed, jealousy worked on her like a slow poison. Presently she could stand it no longer. She was convinced that Kevin had either gone off with Harriet or was to meet her that night.

She rang Lissawn House. Flurry answered. "Is Harry there?" "She is. Will I fetch her?" Maire said no, fudging up some message he could give Harriet.

Her mind was not set at rest. When Kevin had not arrived by 10.30 she knew he must be dallying with Harriet. She bicycled to Lissawn, and crept around in the demesne, listening, peering through the trees.

"And he wasn't there?"

"Please God, he wasn't. They might have been in one of the outhouses, though. I didn't dare go near the house."

"Or the river?" I asked carefully.

"I didn't walk the length of it. I tried to keep hidden among the trees most of the time." Was this said a bit evasively?

"You might have seen her body—on that green spit Flurry fished from the first day I met you."

Maire shuddered. "Was that where?—I didn't know. I wasn't close to that bit of the river. Oh, Dominic, I feel so ashamed of myself. Spying after Kevin. I must have been mad that night."

"So you saw nobody at all?"

"Nobody. And heard nothing. Wait now—as I was cycling back, I saw a drunk fella ahead, only a few hundred yards from the town. I didn't recognise him—my bicycle lamp isn't very good. Then I saw the fella was reeling about in the road. I didn't dare pass him, so I waited a couple of minutes till he'd gone into the town."

"You ought to tell Concannon."

Maire looked at me in consternation. "You mean, he was the murderer?"

"Well, some drunken tramp might have wandered into the demesne—tried to rape her. That's the sort of man Concannon'd be looking for."

"Oh, I could never tell the superintendent. What'd he think of me at all, after telling him such lies."

"You wouldn't want an innocent man hanged for Harriet's murder."

"I wouldn't want anyone hanged for it, God forgive me."

"I told you, the people here think I did it. Concannon probably thinks so too."

Maire glanced at me timidly. "They're fools then. Why should Mr. Concannon put it on you, for goodness' sake?"

"Surely you know?" I said roughly.

After a moment's pause, she answered. "Well, there's been talk, I give you that."

"Talk?"

"We, Kevin and I, thought—we heard you were a bit sweet on Harriet."

"'Sweet!'" I exploded. "Good God, I was passionately in love with her. Sorry. But I can't stand any more of this Irish——"

"So she got you too. Poor Dominic. Never mind now."

I found myself in tears. Any sympathetic voice could do it to me. "She *wasn't* wicked, Maire. Believe me, she wasn't," I quavered. She held my head against her for a minute. Then,

"You must have some food. No, not with the children. I'll bring in a tray for you. Wait while I get you something.'

Maire left me alone in the room. I could hear the voices of the children chattering next door. I thought of Flurry's desire to have a child; and the night I had left Harriet to her fate by the river. I thought of Maire, wandering in the demesne, wild with suspicion and jealousy. Lucky she had not seen me or heard our voices.

But perhaps she *had* seen Harriet, after I'd left her— seen her naked there by the river, and in a fury of jealousy attacked her. No, that was ridiculous. A woman does not go out armed with a penknife against another woman. Or does she? But surely Maire would not have told me about her visit to the demesne that night if she had a worse thing than jealousy on her conscience? I wondered would she confess to Father Bresnihan when he returned. He would be bound by the seal of the confessional; but he would tell Maire it was her duty to let Concannon know of her movements that night.

Kevin was another matter. So practical, efficient a man to let his car run out of petrol? It would be a good cover for an assignation with Harriet. No, that was absurd; she wouldn't have made assignations with both of us; and he could hardly have gone to the Lissawn just on the chance of finding her there. But perhaps, sensing that I was going to throw her over, she *had* arranged for Kevin to meet her there after I left—perhaps even for a confrontation between us. She loved to arouse jealousy: she was a primitive woman in that way. Suppose Kevin had been watching her and me from behind the trees? I had not made love to her. But there was quite enough in the scene to provoke his bitterest jealousy. Kevin was a physical coward, Flurry had told me. He would not dare to confront me, perhaps: but after I had left her——?

If he had had a brainstorm then, sweeping away his usual circumspection? I imagined Harriet mocking him for his cowardice, exasperating his nerve till he pulled out the knife and struck insensately at the body I had stolen from him. I knew all too well how she could get under a man's skin.

But the blood. He must have got some on his clothes. Maire would have seen it when he returned. The police had searched the house. Wait a minute, though. Kevin was a calculating man. He would not murder in hot blood. He would strip for her, and plunge in the river afterwards to wash away the stains. Which Concannon no doubt suspected *I* had done. I saw Kevin's shark-mouth bending over her, and the knife upraised. I shuddered through my whole body.

Maire came in with a tray. "I've rung Flurry. He'll be over any moment on his motorbike. Now you must eat something, Dominic. You look exhausted."

She sat with me till Flurry arrived. I told him about the boycott.

"Where's Kevin?"

"He'll not be back till to-morrow," said Maire. "He went to Dublin."

"Never here when he's wanted. C'mon then, Dominic. I'll fix them myself."

I thanked Maire, and followed him out of the house. A few corner-boys glared at me from the other side of the street, but they didn't dare open their mouths with Flurry there. We went to Leesons Store first, Flurry pushing his bike beside me. A fine mist of rain was falling. In his old trench-coat Flurry looked formidable.

"Where's Brian?" he demanded of the assistant.

"He's not available," said the man.

"He'd better be. Go fetch him. Jump to it, boy."

The assistant went behind the scenes. The shop was empty but for us two. The manager appeared.

"What's all this about Mr. Eyre being refused supplies?"

"Sure it's no doing of mine, Flurry. Mr. Kevin said——"

"To hell with Mr. Kevin!"

"I'd lose my job, Flurry, if——"

"You'll lose something more if you turn obstinate on me."

"Well, if you'll take the responsibility."

"I'll take it all right," said Flurry grimly.

I repeated my order. We conveyed the carton, on the saddle of Flurry's bike, to Sean's garage where I had left my car.

"Fill it up," ordered Flurry when Sean appeared. "No, not *my* tank, Mr. Eyre's."

Sean gave him a shamefaced look. " Well now, Flurry, it's like this," he began.

" Be damn to what it's like. D'you sell petrol outa that pump or don't you?" Flurry's eyes were hard as chips of granite. Where was the easy-going, flabby man I had known?

" If *you* say so." Sean gave him a puzzled look, and filled my tank.

" That's better. And don't let me hear any more of this nonsense. I think we'd best have a drink after that, Dominic."

We crossed the street to the Colooney. Haggerty's ruddy face paled as we strode into the bar.

" I hear you refused my friend a drink just now, Desmond."

" I did," said the manager, trying to brazen it out.

" Well, now you'll give him one. On the house."

" I have a bit of a problem here, Flurry. It's not that I——"

" Hold your whisht! You'll have a worse problem on your hands if——"

" I'll ring Mr. Kevin first, and tell him there's been some mistake."

" You can't," I said. "He's in Dublin."

Haggerty looked nervously round the bar. But the other two occupants had slid out after a glance at Flurry, whose hands were in the pockets of his macintosh trench coat.

" Well then, as a favour to you, Flurry——"

" No, no. You have the wrong idea, my brave boyo." The big man's voice had turned gentle as syrup. " My friend, Mr. Eyre, is doing *you* a favour by drinking your whiskey. And don't put any more water in it than there is already in the bottle." Flurry's voice rose to a bellow. " Get on with it or I'll break your neck!"

" Now that's no way to be talking, Flurry." But, at a

movement of Flurry's huge hands, Haggerty shrank back and set about filling a couple of glasses.

When we went out again, I tried to thank him. Flurry brushed it aside. "When the Mayor's away, the mice can play. Maybe they'll make me deputy-mayor. I wish I knew what the hell Kevin was at. Of course, he'd do it in a roundabout way. Just a word dropped here and there—'I wonder do we have a right to serve Mr. Eyre, in view of' etc. etc. A nod's as good as a wink from him. He has half the town in his pocket. Well, you'd best sail in convoy a while longer. I'll follow you up to my house. I've things to tell you."

We were in the sitting-room at Lissawn House. I had not been there since Harriet's death. The room was cool, though the day was warm outside; and her belongings still strewn about made it seem the more deserted, the more lifeless. It was strange to see Flurry, though, moving around it with a new decisiveness, as though her death had given him a fresh lease of life. He had entirely broken through the abject despair it had put him in at first.

Against all likelihood, I felt at ease with him; and this deepened the unreality of my situation.

"I never trusted that fella Haggerty," he was saying: "he's a jackal. Not that my brother's any class of lion. Now, before Seamus comes in, I'd best tell you what I prodded out of him the other day. He it was shot your hat off from behind the bushes. He only wanted to fright you off."

And left the warning note in my cottage too, I thought.

"He's a loyal man. You and Harry had him worried—you know what I mean—and he thought he was protecting my interests. He wasn't trying to kill you, only warn you off. Will you forgive him?"

"Of course. Though *I'm* not the man who ought to be forgiving anyone," I replied miserably.

"That's all right then."

"Flurry, the way you've treated me since—it's all beyond me. You seem the only person here who doesn't suspect me of——"

"Ah, don't deceive yourself about that, Dominic. You used to think I was a soft man, gone to seed, didn't you now? Maybe you were in the right of it. But things have changed. In the Trouble, I had the execution of some of the Tans; but I never allowed it till I'd proved their crimes against them. I like you, Dominic," he went on with a steely glance at me. "But if I proved it was you who killed Harry, you'd get no mercy from me."

"Yes," I said. "I know that. I accept it."

"I used to think you a poor sort of thing. But I've changed my opinion: you've a real bit of spunk in you. Come in and sit down, Seamus. I've been rescuing Dominic. They put a boycott on him in the town. Did you know that?"

"I heard tell of it yesterday."

"My brother won't be best pleased when he hears I've stopped it. No more loans from the Mayor," said Flurry with a harsh laugh. "But why did he do it?—tell me that."

"First he wanted Mr. Eyre in Joyce's cottage, so he could keep him under his eye. Now he's trying to drive him out of the place altogether," said Seamus. "It doesn't make sense to me at all."

"Was it he who tried to have me drowned?"

I intercepted a look between Seamus and Flurry. "It might have been," said the latter, "though I don't like to think it of my own brother. If he thought you were a danger to him—but how could you be?"

"A bloody queer way to set about it," said Seamus. "Sure why couldn't he have Mr. Eyre knocked on the head and finished in the cottage?"

"Perhaps he's superstitious—didn't want my blood on

his hands. It'd be O.K. if the sea did the murder for him,"
I replied. The light-hearted suggestion was received with
greater gravity than it deserved.

"Mr. Eyre could be in the right of it."

"Oh, come off it, Seamus. I wasn't being serious. Even
an Irishman is not as superstitious as all that."

"I wouldn't put it past Kevin to think that way," said
Flurry. "But I don't believe he meant more than to give
Dominic the fright of his life."

I stared at him. "Well, that's a new idea!"

"Seamus and I have been putting our heads together.
That place where Father Bresnihan found you is not a true
quicksand. Your car didn't sink in deep. There wasn't a
spring tide that month—the water only came half-way up
the car, and Sean got it dragged out easy enough after. I
don't say Kevin'd have lamented much if you'd died of
heart-failure when you saw the waves rising up the car at
you, but that's another thing. No, he just wanted you frit
out of the place."

"And silenced," put in Seamus.

"Silenced? But——"

"You'd heard something that night was a danger to him.
He wanted you out of the country, Mr. Eyre. And he
wanted you to realise that, if you passed on this information
he believed you had, it would be the worse for you."

"I don't get it, Seamus."

"It was a last warning. If you did not clear out and keep
silence when you got home, he'd have you followed to England, and dealt with there. It wouldn't be the first time
the I.R.A. took vengeance on an informer who'd left this
country. He wanted you to have a taste of his power, so
you'd leave him alone."

"But I hadn't heard anything."

"How could he be sure of that?"

"Concannon doesn't agree with you there," said Flurry.

" He was asking me a drift of questions about my brother—trying to find out if I knew anything about Kevin's political activities. Well, I don't. And I wouldn't betray him if I did. Concannon's a deep fellow, though. He has Kevin worried, that I know."

" Maire told me just now her husband thinks he's being followed," I said.

" Is that so? I'll have to have a talk with him. Whatever he's up to, he'd better lay off it awhile. Have you heard anything more, Seamus?"

" I have not."

" Seamus is my eyes and ears, Dominic. He's been searching the length and breadth of the country, if he can get a hint of what Kevin's up to."

" If I could find the man he was talking to that night Mr. Eyre overheard them—— But I can't discover hair nor hoof of him. I did hear he might have been at the horse show where Mrs. Flurry took a toss, but——"

" Wait now," I said excitedly. " I saw a fellow there making a sign to Kevin. I thought he looked a bit furtive."

" Can you describe him?"

I tried to. But I had only caught the one glimpse of him, and in no particular had he stood out from the rest of the crowd.

" He could have been just a fella laying a bet for Kevin," said Flurry. " Maire's terrible down on betting: she watches Kevin like a hawk to see he doesn't have a flutter behind her back."

" Your brother'd only bet on a certainty, anyway," remarked Seamus sourly.

" That's true of the races. But he has a powerful ambition on him. He'd take long odds if he saw the chance of something coming home that'd set him up high. Isn't that so, Seamus?"

" It is."

There was a long silence. At last Flurry said, "Harry never trusted him, God rest her soul."

Well, I thought, she'd not have to trust a man to get into bed with him. Not Harriet. For her, it would add spice to the affair. But might we not all be wrong about the attacks upon me and the murder of Harriet? Was not jealousy behind them?

Yet how could I suggest this to Flurry? He'd said that he wouldn't have minded Harriet going to bed with his own brother, if it made her happy. But that was in the first wildness of grief. Flurry never meant it to be taken seriously. And he was a changed man now: if I told him that Harriet had confessed to me there'd been a liaison between her and his brother, and that Maire had suspected it, I'd be signing Kevin's death warrant.

Chapter 11

At midday on the morrow, Flurry and I were waiting inside
the gate of the Church of Ireland graveyard. Maire was with
us, but not Kevin: she made some excuse for his absence,
which I did not take in. A fine rain had begun to fall; but
it did not discourage the groups of townsfolk standing in
the lane outside, silent, not menacing now—Flurry and I
had passed through them with no trouble—but appraising
and patient in their curiosity. I felt like a beast in a cage.

Three uniformed Gardai stood by the gate. A car drove
up, and Concannon got out: giving Flurry and me a preoccupied nod, he passed into the church. Murderers, they
say, feel compelled to attend the funeral of their victim.
Was Concannon here to observe my reactions?

I looked round at the unkempt graveyard. Tombstones
stuck up like teeth, discoloured and dishonoured, from the
rank grass. I wanted to think about Harriet, to savour this
finality and my grief: but my mind threw up no picture of
her—only a grotesque thought: after the autopsy, would
they have put back the embryo into her and stitched her up?

I became aware of Flurry beside me, standing absolutely
immobile, like a granite rock. It was thus that he would
have faced an execution squad. No flinching, no prayers
perhaps. I could not connect this hard man with the Flurry
I had known for three months. It came to me in a revelation
that I felt towards him now as a father figure: I had a son's
sense of guilt, no less for my past misunderstanding of him
than for the wrong I had done him: I felt bound to him.

At that moment the hearse arrived. The crowd drew back
to the far side of the lane, the men and women crossing

themselves. Flurry's huge hand gripped my arm—to give comfort or receive it? I felt the weight of the ordeal he was suffering.

The bearers shouldered the coffin and carried it through the gate. That hideous, polished box with its hideous brass handles. It looked much too small to contain Harriet. With a discreet gesture, the master of ceremonies (I could only think of him so) indicated that we should follow the coffin. Flurry, head up, walked steadily behind it: Maire and I came after him.

The church was bleak and dank inside, the service mercifully short. Maire looked covertly about her to see how these things were done in the Protestant persuasion. Flurry's eyes, I believe, never left the coffin for an instant. I remembered that day Harriet and I had seen the funeral cortège moving over the strand: the parson's words meant as little to me as had the screaming gulls then: I wanted to recall Harriet, in all the outrageous vitality of her flesh, for the last time before she went underground. But all I could see was a dim reflection of my face in the coffin's wood.

Then we were moving out of the church again. Not twenty yards away was a heap of earth, a gash in the grass. The coffin was lowered into it, tilting awkwardly at one moment. The last words were said, the handfuls of dust thrown in. Flurry took a rose from one of the wreaths and dropped it on the coffin. His lips moved silently. I noticed Concannon looking steadily at him. Then Flurry walked away.

Maire, putting away her handkerchief, gave me a strangely solicitous look and took my arm, guiding me through the tussocks of wet grass to the gate, as if I were an invalid out for his first walk after a dangerous illness. I became aware of the tears trickling down my cheeks.

"Never mind, Dominic," she said. "It's all over now."

A hand opened the gate for us. It was Concannon's. All

over for *Harriet*, I thought. The groups of people in the lane made way for us. Last time it had been Flurry convoying me, to-day it was Maire. I felt utterly drained of emotion: my eyes saw the world as two-dimensional; the lane, the dripping trees, the houses of Charlottestown might have been cut out of cardboard.

I heard myself say to Maire, " She should have had a fine day for it."

" Won't you come in a little and have some brandy?"

" It's kind of you, Maire, but I'm taking Flurry home."

He was waiting for me by my car, talking to Concannon, who had got ahead of us. Before we moved off, Concannon took me aside and asked me to make myself available at the cottage this afternoon. There seemed to be some change in his manner towards me, though I could not put my finger on it exactly.

Flurry was silent on the way back. Only when I had dropped him at Lissawn House did he beg me to spend the evening with him. " You'd be doing me a favour, Dominic. I can't face being alone to-night. We'll have a wake, the two of us. Will y' do that for me?"

How could I refuse?

Back at the cottage, I opened a tin of tongue and ate it with bread and butter. I was on edge at the thought of yet another interview with Concannon. To calm myself, I decided I would write to my mother and tell her something of what had been happening. I had meant to earlier, and even inserted a fresh sheet of paper in my typewriter; but before I'd written a word, something had turned up to prevent me. I must have taken the sheet out again, though I had no recollection of doing so, for it was not in the typewriter now.

At three o'clock, Concannon arrived. This time he was alone, which gave me a certain sense of relief. His manner, too, seemed less official.

"You must be feeling bad, Mr. Eyre, with the funeral and all. Still, duty's duty," he began, peeling off his raincoat and settling himself on the narrow window-seat. "I'm told you and Flurry Leeson are thick as thieves just now."

"I'm very grateful to him," I said cautiously. "He's saved me from starvation."

"Has he now?" Concannon's intelligent eyes probed at me through the dim little room. I told him about the boycott. He appeared interested rather than surprised, and made me describe in detail the forms this boycott had taken.

"Ah well. Very unpleasant for you. The people here are terrible down on foreigners," he said cosily. "But you're all right now?"

"I don't believe the people here did it spontaneously. They'd had instructions, if you ask me."

"Who from?"

"Kevin Leeson. Who else? Didn't the police know anything about it?"

"Kevin Leeson? That's a grave allegation to be making about him. Have you any evidence? Have you faced him with it?"

"No. It only happened yesterday, and he was away somewhere. I did have a talk with his wife, though. She took me in when they were going to mob me."

"I see. She knew nothing of the boycott?"

"I don't think so. But if she did, she wouldn't have joined in. She's a decent woman."

"So she is, so she is. Now about yourself, Mr. Eyre. Do you want to change the statement you made to me?"

"The statement?"

"About your movements the night Harriet Leeson was killed?"

"So I'm still your chief suspect?"

"You haven't answered my question."

"No. Why should I change it?" I was indignant—at myself for having lied to the superintendent. But I must go through with it now. "If I'd crept out that night and killed Harriet, I'd hardly confess it to you. I did not kill her."

"But you did creep out." Concannon's voice tilted up at the end.

"No," I said firmly.

"It's a pity, then. You might have heard something, seen something, which would give us a clue."

I stayed silent.

"You're so friendly with Flurry Leeson now," he went on in the tones of one, as they say, thinking aloud. "You owe him a great deal, Mr. Eyre, and I'm not talking about the boycott chiefly."

"What do you mean?"

"You owe him a great deal," said Concannon with sudden brutality, "for lending you his wife."

"That's between him and me."

"So you've confessed to him about your liaison."

He had trapped me there. "Yes, I have."

"And he took it well?" There was a satirical edge to Concannon's voice. I had the sense of being subtly man-œuvred, like a chess-man.

"He understood. Flurry's a remarkable man—I've come to realise that."

"There's no jealousy in his make-up at all? He must be a saint then. Doesn't he even feel jealous about your having made his wife pregnant?"

Concannon had turned on the heat with a vengeance.

"He doesn't suspect that," I replied wretchedly. "I don't know if it's true myself."

What I must never tell Concannon was that I'd also confessed to Flurry about having been with Harriet the night she was murdered. The superintendent's next remark surprised me.

"I'm sure you're a great student of human nature. You couldn't write novels else."

"I suppose I am."

"But maybe you've a deal to learn still. About primitive people—people like us savage Irishmen. We're a devious lot, you know. We've had centuries' practice concealing our grudges against the English."

"I don't see what——"

"An Irishman could conceal even his bitterest jealousy, till the moment comes to——"

Concannon's voice faded away. Then he began again. "What I'm saying is, Flurry may have had you on a string all this time. When he had final proof of your affair with his wife, he put an end to her. It was the murder of a jealous man."

"No, no, no!" I burst out. "Flurry—you've got him utterly wrong."

"He had the motive. He had the opportunity—Father Bresnihan had just left him. He found his wife naked by the river, waiting for some other man. Wouldn't that make you see red?"

"I simply don't believe it. He'd have killed *me*, if he was that sort of man—killed us both."

"Don't you see how clever it is of him to take up with you like he's done since. It's aimed to show what a forgiving fellow he is. How could a jealous man behave like that? It casts suspicion right away from him."

"Are you serious?"

"I'm dead serious, Mr. Eyre."

"But you searched Lissawn House."

"If you're thinking of blood-stained clothes, whoever did it must have done it stripped and then plunged into the river. Flurry. Or you, Mr. Eyre."

My heart sagged again. "Why don't you arrest me then and get it over with?" I exclaimed. "I don't like this cat-and-mouse——"

"And I don't like murder," said Concannon formidably. "Nor would I like charging the wrong man."

"So it's between Flurry and me now, is it? You should look a bit farther afield."

"Where will I look?" he asked mildly.

The idea of Flurry being under such suspicion made me indiscreet. I did not want Maire hurt, but I could not bear Flurry to be thought guilty.

"If it's a jealous man you're looking for, why don't you pay a bit more attention to Kevin?"

Concannon's face took on a guarded expression. I realised I was doing just what a guilty man would do—try to draw suspicion on someone else. But it was too late to draw back.

"Harriet more or less admitted to me that Kevin had been her lover. I've told you that already. Did you realise he was very near the Lissawn demesne when she was murdered?"

"Was he now?"

"Good God man, aren't you interested?"

"How did you know this?"

I recounted all that Maire had told me, about that night— all except her own wanderings in the demesne—this would have been too gross a betrayal of confidence. Concannon heard out my deductions; not very enthusiastically, but no professional likes an amateur muscling in on his own territory.

"So, you see, that car journey of his should be investigated. If he falsified the times, it would——"

"I'll look after that."

The sun, in the unpredictable Irish way, had burst out from the hopeless day and was shining slantwise through the window. I could see Concannon gazing at me, with that guarded look turned faintly quizzical now on his austere face. He might have been a Jesuit receiving the notions of a not-too-bright neophyte on a theological question.

"Well, if that's all you——"

"Ah no. You've been a great help, Mr. Eyre. I'm grateful. But you know, if it's jealousy in it, we have another candidate."

"Have we?"

"Maire Leeson was jealous enough of her husband to go stravagueing the countryside after him just because he was an hour or two late."

"Oh, for heaven's sake, you don't think *she* would kill anyone?"

"And why not? I got the impression, when I questioned her, that she was a repressed woman—but with hidden fires banked down, you know. Her husband is too cold a man to lose his head and commit a crime of passion." Concannon paused to light one of his rare cigarettes. "I believe you're the same, Mr. Eyre, at bottom."

"Thank you very much!" I replied, inordinately vexed. At least, I had not told him Maire's movements that night after waiting about on the main road. Then I remembered the drunken tramp she had seen. Should I divulge this? No: it was just the story a woman would make up to divert suspicion, had she herself killed Harriet. And I trusted Seamus to unearth this tramp, if anyone could.

We talked desultorily five minutes more. Then Concannon rose to go.

"How much longer do I have to stay here?"

"Till I've ended my investigations, Mr. Eyre," he replied neutrally.

"And when will that be?"

He shrugged.

"But damn it, I may be the next target."

"You'll come to no harm; so long as you're under Flurry Leeson's protection." . . .

A few hours later I was in the fishing room at Lissawn House. Flurry and I were already well away with the whiskey. It was a queer sort of wake, the night *after* the funeral, in an empty house, two mourners talking in fuddled tones about the woman who should have set them at each other's throats. Flurry was drinking to forget her: I drank to obliterate the suspicion Concannon had planted in my mind, that Flurry might have murdered her.

"What was that fella Concannon after?" he said, picking the thought out of my mind.

"He thinks you could have killed her. The silly sod."

"Does he now? Well, he'd have the right."

"I told him it was bloody ridiculous."

Flurry hefted a rod, then laid it back on the table beside him. "He was trying to drag something out of you?"

"He was. And to make me admit I'd been with Harriet the night she——"

"But you didn't?"

"You're the only person who'll ever know that, Flurry."

"And I'm not telling," he replied, and loosed an uninhibited belch. "It's queer, us two sitting here talking about her. Bloody queer. If you read it in a book, you'd not believe it. Ah well, women are the devil—God rest her soul."

At some stage in the evening, Flurry brought in bread and cheese. At another, he inveighed against the reporters who had been pestering him. "There's no privacy to-day at all at all. Them fellas'll be peering over the recording angel's shoulder at the Day of Judgment to see what he has written down."

"They won't read anything very bad about you, Flurry."

"Except murder, maybe," he said sombrely.

I was suddenly sobered. "But it was in war you killed."

"To hell with the Tans! I'm not talking about them." He gave me a cunning look. "And I'm not talking about Harry either, whatever Mr. Bloody Concannon may think. It's the fella who killed her. I'll have his blood on my hands."

"Why don't you leave him to the Law?"

Flurry spat into the fireplace. "The Law?—the Law! I'll not let him slip me that way."

"Flurry, you're tight. You'll think better of it as time goes on. D'you want to be hanged yourself?"

"I want to lay my hands on that fella. Sure what else have I to live for, now Harry's gone?" His watering eyes turned to me. "What sort of a man d'you think I am?"

"I think you're a lazy man, an easy-going man at heart. You have a romantic urge to violence; but violence is against your nature. So you have to plunge into it blindfold. You're a soft-hearted man really, and you resent that—you want an excuse for turning your heart to stone."

Flurry had gazed at me with increasing astonishment during this analysis. "Well, for God's sake! Never did I hear such desperate crap. Dominic, you're the one is tight. I can't make head nor tail of what you're saying."

"Nor can I, now you cast doubt upon it. But tell me this —I wouldn't have asked it if I wasn't drunk—why didn't you strangle me when I—when I told you my secret?"

"Secret?"

"When I told you I'd been with Harriet the night she was murdered?"

There was a long pause. Flurry seemed to be assembling his thoughts. "I nearly did, you know. But I'm not such a fool as I look. I worked it out for myself that no guilty man would dare make that confession to me and put his life in *my* hands. Sure you didn't have to tell me that part of it, did you now?"

"But——"

"Wait a while. In the bad times once, I had to question a man we suspected of betraying two of his friends to the Auxiliaries. He denied it. He put on a great show of grief for his friends—they'd been tortured and shot. But it didn't ring true. I knew in my bones it was not honest grief. Yours was. And yours felt like an act of true contrition. Now I'm talking like Father Bresnihan. To hell with it! This is a bloody dismal wake. We should have a song. D'you know 'The Boys of Wexford'?"

So I sang as much of it as I could remember, Flurry beating time on the table and joining raucously in the chorus. I went on to "The Harp That Once," and then found myself singing "She Moved Through the Fair," which reduced Flurry to tears. At some point Seamus must have come in, for I remember him supporting Flurry's sagging figure and bellowing voice in some revolutionary songs.

Finally Flurry collapsed into a chair. "That's better. That's more like it. He's a grand voice, hasn't he, Seamus?"

"He has."

"No bloody keening about this wake. Did y' ever hear the keening, Dominic?"

"No."

"A god-awful din. Like a pack of wolves baying the moon. It'd freeze your bones."

"When did you ever hear a pack of wolves, Flurry?" asked Seamus.

"I'll hear it when the bailiffs come."

"Which reminds me——"

"Ah, get out with you, Seamus! I'll have no long faces at this wake. Drink up. D'you know, boys, it's the first time I've been able to get drunk since Harry—— I must have a drink on that."

I laboriously thought back. It was only the fourth day since Harriet's death. It seemed an age.

"Well, we all loved her. To Harry, rest her soul!"

We drank solemnly.

"And now I drink to Dominic. May the devil fly away with the roof of the house where you and I are not welcome!"

"And here's to Seamus," I said. "Seamus, I bequeath you my Connemara tweed hat. I can't say fairer than that."

"I take it kindly, Mr. Eyre."

"You're welcome."

"That terrible old lid?" said Flurry. "Is that the best you can do for him? Sure there's not anny old tinker'd be seen dead in it."

"Which reminds me——"

"Ah, shut up, Seamus!"

"No. Let the man speak. He has something of moment to connumicate—communicate, I should say."

"I couldn't find hide nor hair of that tinker Mrs. Kevin says she saw. No one in the town set eyes on him."

"Why should they? They'd be all in bed, that time of night," said Flurry.

"And so should I be." I looked at my watch. It said nearly one o'clock. I rose, only to fall against the table.

"Dominic, you're drunk."

"Will I walk you home, Mr. Eyre?"

"You will not," roared Flurry. "He's staying here the night."

"Oh but——"

"I'll take no denial. D'ye hear me?"

Seamus winked at me. "The commandant'll take no denial."

"All right then. Thank you, Flurry."

"Tha's better. For a West Britisher, I don't mind you at all. Drink up now and shame the devil."

It was nearly two o'clock before we retired. Flurry led me to a small room next his own. "There's something wrong with that bed, me boy," he said, gazing bemusedly at it. "What is it now?"

I cudgelled my reeling brain. "There's no bedclothes on it."

"By God, you have it."

He reappeared with a bundle of sheets and blankets in his arms. He and I weaved around the bed, making it up.

"Is there anything else you'll be needing?"

I thought hard again. "Yes. Pyjamas."

He returned with a pair of his own. "Good night now, and thank you for keeping me company to-day. Sleep well."

I didn't. Unaired sheets are the worst somnifuges. I felt the damp creeping into my bones, as I tossed and turned. Presently I threw off the sheets and wrapped myself in a blanket. But all the liquor I had drunk over-stimulated my brain. I lay there with my eyes open, first to prevent the walls circling round me, and then, after I had them quietened down, thinking of all the times with Harriet, of the mystery I was caught up in, of Flurry's strange personality and incalculable behaviour. Was I lying in bed next door to a murderer? Surely not. He was a man whose simplicity baffled me: but he was not a simple-minded man. He had the intuition, I reflected, of a first-class military leader; and the ruthlessness of a guerrilla. But one thing was sure—he had loved Harriet with a love which transcended jealousy.

The uncurtained window appeared to grow light. Dawn already. I lit the candle and looked at my watch. Only five to three. I went to the window. At first it seemed as if some distant trees in the demesne were on fire. Then I saw the flames were well beyond them. And at that moment I heard running feet on the avenue. A man hurdled the stile into the garden, shouting.

"Joyce's is burning! Ring the brigade!"

I rushed into Flurry's room. He was snoring loud. But

at the touch of my hand (I was to remember this later), he came full awake.

" Ring the brigade, Flurry. My cottage is on fire."

He was half-way down the stairs before I had collected my own wits. The man was banging on the front door. When I let him in, I saw he was the neighbour of mine who lived a hundred yards down the lane from me. He was so out of breath, he could not speak at first. I heard Flurry's voice on the telephone at the back of the hall. Then he rushed back. " They'll be on their way. Hallo, Michael. Dominic, throw on your clothes."

It was only then that I noticed he himself had not undressed.

Chapter 12

A few minutes later, running breathlessly, we were at the cottage. A few neighbours stood on the track, admiring the flames. The thatched roof was burning cheerfully, giving off an occasional burst of smoking straws which floated down on our heads. The upper windows had cracked in the heat; the two little bedrooms up there must be red-hot.

"Why the hell can't you lousers do something!" bawled Flurry! "Get a ladder and some buckets!"

"It's no good at all, Mr. Flurry," said a man. "Sure the place must have gone up like a bomb. It was a raging furnace when we arrived."

I made a dash for the door, unlocked it and plunged in. The smoke downstairs blinded me and the heat was hellish, but I groped my way to the table, snatched up my MSS and diary, and staggered out. A few moments later, the upper floor collapsed with a crash. Smoke and sparks billowed out through the open door, and a torch of flame shot up thirty feet above the room. I unlocked my car door, and the men helped me push the car out of range of the conflagration.

A few minutes later, two antiquated fire-engines arrived. Jets of water were directed at the roof, which hissed at them with derision. I began to shiver uncontrollably. Flurry, excitement in his eye, gripped my arm.

"That's a monster of a blaze. Aren't you glad you slept the night with me?"

"Why was it the top floor caught? I don't understand it."

The other appliance which had arrived could not use its ladder against this inferno.

"If there's anyone there," said the chief fire officer, "he's destroyed."

" The cottage was empty."

" Did you keep much petrol in it? That's not a natural blaze."

" No. I didn't keep any."

" It looks like arson to me, then. We'll have a search to-morrow, when we've got the place damped down. Though it'd be a miracle if we found anything. Is this gentleman a friend of yours, Mr. Leeson?" added the officer, with a somewhat suspicious look at me.

" He is, and I'm taking him home to bed. He's worn out, can't you see?"

I drove Flurry back to Lissawn House. " That was a great end to the wake," he said heartlessly.

" Oh, marvellous."

" Kevin'll be wild, losing his cottage and five pound a week."

" A month. But look here, Flurry, not a soul knew I'd decided to spend the night with you. If someone did set the place on fire, he'd assume I was in it. And how would he get in? The door was locked."

" He'd have a key then." Flurry did not seem to grasp the implications of this.

" And locked up again behind him? To make sure I couldn't get out? The windows are far too small to climb through."

" You must have left something burning then."

" But I wasn't there after Concannon left, in the afternoon. I'd not lit the lamp. The turf fire was out."

" Be easy, Dominic. Keefe'll sort it when he has the fire put out. Go to bed now. You're dropping."

And believe it or not, damp sheets and excitement and all, I must have gone to sleep as soon as my head touched the pillow.

I was awoken at 9.30 by the telephone bell ringing downstairs. Presently Flurry appeared. "Concannon wants a word with you." I crawled down to the instrument, my head splitting. The superintendent's first words did not clear up my sense of total disorientation.

"Good morning, Mr. Eyre. So you thought better of it."

"*Thought better?* What on earth are you talking about?"

There was a brief silence. "You'll be at Lissawn House at two o'clock? I'm busy this morning."

"I could hardly be anywhere else, now someone has burnt down my cottage."

"I'll be over there. You and Mr. Leeson had better not lose sight of each other till I come."

"And what's the meaning of that sinister remark?" I asked sourly, but Concannon had already rung off.

Flurry was frying eggs and bacon in the kitchen.

"What on earth's Concannon raving about?"

"He asked when I'd seen you last, and I told him you were asleep upstairs, worn out with booze and excitement." Flurry was in great shape. "It seemed to knock him all of a heap. And what did he tell you?"

"To keep an eye on *you*—he's turning up after lunch."

"Are you insured, Dominic?"

"Do you mean my possessions or my life?"

This caused him to laugh uproariously. He was certainly his old self again. "You're a great joker," he wheezed, in between fits of coughing. "I wouldn't want you to lose the one nor the other."

"I didn't have much in the cottage. A few books and clothes. Oh, and my binoculars. It's a nuisance about the typewriter: but I rescued my MSS."

"That's what you care about most," he ventured, almost shyly.

"I suppose so. But I'm beginning to think it's a worthless novel."

"Ah well, you've your life before you. C'mon now and

eat up. If you can keep the first mouthful down, you're all right."

He gave me a cup of coffee laced with whiskey. "This'll restore you. A hair of the dog, as the saying is." He looked out of the window. "We'll have a cloud-burst before the day's end. So we can fish the river to-morrow, please God."

After breakfast I went out for a stroll in the demesne. I felt better, but my head still throbbed and the air was thunderous. A weight of indigo cloud was building up over the mountains inland. My feet took me, as if magnetised, to that green spot by the Lissawn. So dark was the day that I could imagine Harriet ghosting towards me through the trees in her white night-dress.

The water was low and sullen. Rocks stood up out of it like tombstones. Flurry had told me that, the day after Harriet's death, police in waders were searching that stretch of the Lissawn. In those days there were no skin-divers or metal-detectors—not in the West of Ireland, anyway. And the pool where he so often cast his fly was pretty deep. So, if the knife was there, it had not been discovered.

I heard a car coming slowly up the avenue, and soon recognised it through the trees. I ran to cut it off, arriving neatly as Kevin climbed out. He turned round, and there I was. If I had hoped he might, in the shock, betray himself, it was a failure. He did not grow pale or start back.

"How are you?" he said, gripping my hand warmly.

"None the worse for being alive."

"That's a terrible thing to have happened. It's the mercy of providence you weren't sleeping there last night."

"Oh, you've heard about the fire."

"Keefe told me—the fire brigade chief. Then I drove past on my way here. The place is gutted. Only the walls standing."

"Has Keefe found out how it started?"

"He's investigating. Of course he'll have to call in the

insurance company's fire assessors. But it's you I'm worried about: I'm afraid you must have lost everything. Anything I can lend you, just call on me—you'll be wanting a replacement for your typewriter."

"That's very kind of you."

By this time we were in the house. Flurry was in his fishing room, tying flies. "Hallo, Kevin," he said, not looking up, "so you're burning down your own houses now. You might have warned us."

"I don't like that class of joke at all. Don't you realise Dominic might have——"

"Been fried to a crisp? Yes, I see your point: as the actress said to the bishop."

"This is no time to be making foul jokes, Flurry. I——"

"Well, what did you come here for?"

"To inquire after Dominic, of course. He's had a dreadful ordeal."

"That's true enough, Kevin. What's changed your mind?"

"I don't understand you."

"If you're so solicitous about him, why did you put the boycott on him?"

"Damn that for a lie!" Kevin shouted. "I wasn't even in the town when—— You watch what you're saying, he knows damn' well why."

Flurry laid down the cast, and ticked off on his huge fingers each incident of the boycott. "Brigid, Sean, Haggerty, Brian at the store—they're all under your thumb."

"Maybe the people here did take against Mr. Eyre. And brother."

"So it was quite spontaneous?"

"Like the combustion," I said nastily, "at Joyce's cottage."

"Don't talk cod," Kevin burst out furiously. "Everyone in Charlottestown knew about Harriet and Mr. Eyre—

everyone except you, apparently. They'd have a right to suspect he'd murdered her. I don't believe it myself, but ____"

"But you don't object to anyone else believing it. Ah, come off it. What's really worrying you, Kevin? You look like a treed fox."

And he did. There was an uncertainty about his grim, shark-like mouth, a quite uncharacteristic violence in his manner. I got the feeling that he was on the edge of panic.

"I'd like to talk to you alone, Flurry."

"No. Dominic is staying. Two minds are better than one, if there's trouble in it."

There was a pause. "I'm sorry for what I said just now, both of you. I *am* in trouble. You'll hardly believe it, but Superintendent Concannon has nigh acused me of—of the murder. He's been on at me again about the journey I took from Galway. As if I could remember every inch of the way and account for every minute of the night. It's a great trial, when I've so much else on my mind."

"What else?" asked Flurry, gazing straightly at him.

"Oh, business affairs," said Kevin impatiently and, I thought, evasively. "Maire's on at me too."

"Is she now?"

"She thinks I—she's jealous—she had a lunatic idea I'd been—well, a bit sweet on Harriet myself. She said it straight out only the other day. Sure I don't know what way to turn."

"And of course you'd not been consorting with my wife?"

"Don't anger me!"

A single crash of thunder made Kevin start in his chair. It was not repeated, but from now on I could hear a distant thunderstorm bumbling around in the mountains to the east. Flurry had begun tying a fly again: his fingers were amazingly nimble. Without looking up, he said,

"There's something else wrong, Kevin me boy. You may be the great panjandrum in Charlottestown, but you're not the Almighty yet. What've you been getting yourself into?"

His tone was gentle enough, almost appealing. But Kevin, though his long mouth twitched, remained stubbornly silent.

"Well then," continued Flurry. "I'll make a guess at it. You've got yourself involved in some eejut political business, and now you're so far in, you daren't pull out: your associates would be after your blood if you tried to. You and I haven't always seen eye to eye, Kevin. But you're my brother. I wouldn't like to see you prisoned in the Curragh —or worse."

"You fought for Ireland yourself, once," muttered Kevin.

"And a bloody lot of good I did myself!"

"I said 'for Ireland,' not for yourself, Flurry."

Flurry banged his fist impatiently on the table. "So you're set to be another martyr? I don't believe it. Whatever you're in, you're in for what you can get out of it."

"That's a lie! You've always tried to keep me down," said Kevin, flushing. "You've always envied me because I've made good, while you sit about trading on your reputation as a veteran of the Tan War and borrowing money off me and letting your wife kick up her heels——"

"That's enough! Get out! I wash my hands of you."

The two brothers glared at each other. Kevin jumped up and strode out of the room.

Flurry turned back to his casts, forking a fresh one out of a tin box with the three fingers of his maimed hand. "I was too hasty with him, Dominic. That fella riles me, and he always did. I have a firm intention of amendment every time; but then he's apt to throw something at me next time we meet and I lose my temper with him again!"

Gazing past his head out of the window, I saw a suddenly-drawn curtain of rain. The clouds had burst, tipping their burden on to the earth—a sheet as solid as a waterfall.

"That's great," said Flurry. "The water'll be lovely to-morrow."

I wandered into the drawing-room, and absently picked up one from the pile of Harriet's trashy magazines. I reflected once again on Flurry's changed personality since her death. Perhaps his former facetiousness was neither natural to him nor a mask: perhaps it was the attempt of an older man to keep up with a younger woman—to keep her amused and amenable. Had he in a way lowered himself to her own level? out of love and mental indolence? Her death had certainly shaken him out of the indolence. The new Flurry was formidable, like a huge, sleepy, grey tomcat which has rediscovered the speed of its paw.

The bow window showed rain dense as a bead-curtain, the Lissawn seething with it, the montbretia and fuchsia wilting under its onslaught. I felt a fantastic impulse to run out naked into the downpour, as if it could purify me. Instead, I went upstairs and made my bed, then took up the MSS. pages I had rescued and began reading despondently through them. No, it wouldn't do—a wooden, artificial novel. It had been better burnt when the cottage went up—destroyed, like the child Flurry believed to be his, when its mother died.

Flurry, Seamus and I had a scratch meal together—they both seemed preoccupied—and sharp at two o'clock Concannon arrived. Flurry went to let him in, and helped him out of his mac, which had been soaked just running twenty yards from his car to the front door. They came into the drawing-room.

"So you lost your nerve, Mr. Eyre," said Concannon, gazing at me curiously.

"I wish I knew what you're talking about."

He pulled a sheet of paper from his brief-case, and held it up by two corners before my eyes. "This. No, don't touch it, just read it." It was in typescript, with my signature at the bottom.

Dear Mr. Concannon,

This is to let you know I cannot face things any longer. I killed Harriet Leeson. She had been my mistress and was going to have a child by me. I feared the disgrace, and I feared Flurry would kill me when he found out. I made an assignation with her that night. I begged her to release me, but she said if I did not run away with her she would tell her husband about the baby. So I had to silence her. I had brought a knife in case I needed it. I threw it into the river after, and washed her blood off me in the river. I am sorry. I do not deserve to live. I shall go to bed to-night and poison myself. I'll be out of my misery before you get this.

Yours faithfully

Dominic Eyre

"But I never wrote that," I said at last, utterly bewildered.

"It was written on your typewriter—I had a specimen from it a few days ago. And it's your signature, isn't it?"

"It does look like it. It's a forgery, though."

"But you can't forge fingerprints."

"*Fingerprints?*"

"I got the letter by this morning's post. I had it tested. It bears your fingerprints upon it—and no one else's."

I collapsed into a chair, dumbfounded. I thought I was going to faint. Flurry made a move to look at the letter, but Concannon whipped it back into his brief-case. "This is a letter from Mr. Eyre, confessing to the murder of your wife, and saying he's going to commit suicide."

"I'll not believe it."

"Explain the fingerprints then, Mr. Leeson."

Flurry shook his head sadly. I felt desperate: the trap had closed at last. Concannon seemed to be waiting for me to say something, but my throat was dry. Flurry said, "Look here. If it was all true, and Dominic funked it at the last moment, he'd have made a bolt for it by now, knowing he could not stop the letter."

"This sheet of paper, with his signature and prints, out on his own typewriter——"

I broke in excitedly, remembering something. I told Concannon how I'd put a fresh sheet in the machine a few days ago, but not started writing anything—some interruption. And after his visit to the cottage yesterday, I'd noticed it was gone.

"You're not suggesting *I* stole it, I hope."

"Don't be silly."

"When did you last notice it in the machine?" he said humouringly.

"That same morning. Before the funeral. *Funeral!* I was out of the house an hour or more. Somebody could have come in and seen that sheet and known it would have my prints on it and typed that letter."

"An interesting story, Mr. Eyre. It's easy to see you're an imaginative writer."

"It's a bloody lot more sensible than your notions, Concannon," rumbled Flurry.

"Very well, let's take it as a hypothesis. X types the confession and mails it to me. Now he has to arrange for your suicide the same night. Why and how?"

"Because X is the murderer, and this 'confession' and my suicide would put him in the clear," I replied quickly.

"I see. What about the 'how'?"

"Ah, that's an easy one," said Flurry unexpectedly.

"Is it now? All right, you tell me."

"Don't you know Joyce's was fired last night?"

"I thought the idea was that Mr. Eyre should take poison, not burn himself alive," remarked the superintendent satirically. "A very uncomfortable death."

"Don't be a bloody fool, man. Will you hold your whisht till I have it worked out in my mind. Did you ask Keefe what he found?"

"I did."

"Was there the remains of an oil lamp in the wreckage?"

"There was. On the floor. The upper floor had collapsed."

"All right then. If I was going to do the job, will I tell you how I'd set about it? Now don't keep interrupting—it sends my mind astray. I'd be sure Dominic was sound asleep by two o'clock. I'd let myself quietly into the cottage, with a can of petrol maybe. Did you usually bring the lamp up to bed?"

"No. A candle."

Flurry paced up and down the room. "All right. I light the lamp, go carefully up the ladder with it and the can. I overturn the lamp on the floor and throw the petrol over it —maybe a lighted match as well. The whole room goes up. I run down the ladder with the empty can, lock the cottage door so Dominic can't get out, if he has any life left in him, and bob's your uncle."

"All this, though you could see Mr. Eyre was not in the bed at all?"

"How would I see that in the dark? I'd not walk in and prod him, to make sure. I'd just do my stuff with the petrol and the lamp, and get away fast."

"You'd make a fortune at the Abbey," said Concannon, but I could see he was beginning to be impressed. "You've still not allowed for the poison, though. Is Mr. Eyre supposed to have set fire to himself after drinking it?"

"He'd have the lamp by his bedside and knock it over in his dying convulsions," explained Flurry, not without relish, "and set fire to the place accidentally."

"But we'd find no poison in him after," said Concannon, warming to the game.

"Poison in a blackened corpse? You'd never trouble yourselves to look for it. You'd have the confession——"

"Ah, but we would."

"Well, maybe the fella that typed the letter tipped some poison into Dominic's—did you have a glass of water by your bedside?"

"No," I said.

"You took a night-cap regular?"

"Not regularly. Sometimes."

"He could have put some poison in your whiskey and hoped for the best."

"All this is just speculation," said Concannon impatiently. "I'm not saying it couldn't have happened that way. But who is this X you're after building up?"

I was about to speak, but Flurry forestalled me. "Kevin had a key. He was not at the funeral. He believes you suspect him of killing my wife, so he'd have a motive for putting it on Dominic."

"And," I added, "he seems to have typewriters on the brain: he offered just now to replace the one I lost in the fire."

"You have it in for him, Flurry," was the superintendent's comment. "I visited him an hour ago. He declares he was in bed at home all last night, and Mrs. Leeson confirms it."

"She'd be apt to. But Kevin has ones will do his bidding, and well you know it. Did ye ask him where he was at during the funeral?"

"I did not. It'll be investigated. I don't have an army at my disposal."

"But you have enough men to keep me under surveillance," I said, rather bitchily.

Concannon took the point. "I lifted the guard off you a couple of days ago. That was a mistake, I'll grant you. They might have prevented what happened at the cottage."

"If you ask me, you just withdrew them to a little distance, so I'd be lured into making a bolt for it."

Concannon ignored this. He told Flurry he had things to discuss with me in private. Giving me a wink, Flurry withdrew. I felt oddly defenceless without him. The superintendent began to question me at great length about the events of the previous night. What time we had gone to bed? How had we been warned of the fire? Had I been asleep when the news came? And so on, and on.

He elicited from me the information that I'd had no trouble awaking Flurry, and that he'd been fully dressed. "We'd been drinking," I explained. "No doubt he'd fallen into bed without troubling to undress."

"And you say he'd been very pressing for you to spend the night here?"

"Well, he didn't have to press very hard."

Concannon went on asking questions, whose drift I could not yet determine. I gave him my hazy recollections of the post-burial "wake"—the sentimentality, the singing, the boisterousness.

"A queer way to carry on, and your wife just laid in the grave," he said. "Was Seamus not shocked at it all?"

I found myself on the defensive, but for Flurry's sake now.

"Not noticeably," I replied. "Flurry loved her. There's no doubt of that. Why be censorious about the way it took him?"

Concannon was a bit nettled by this. Back we went to the question and answer. Finally, he said,

"So you couldn't be *sure* that Flurry didn't slip out of the house after you'd gone to bed last night?"

"Good God, you can't suppose it was *he* set fire to the cottage? Why in heaven's name should he do that?"

"To incriminate his brother."

"You must be out of your mind, Superintendent."

"Seamus was not at the funeral. He could have typed your 'confession,' and mailed it. He'd do anything for Flurry."

"But——"

"I saw a cartoon once," he went on easily. "There was one ruffian stalking a fellow with a knife. And unbeknownst to him, he was being stalked with a knife by a second ruffian."

"Now isn't that an exciting story, kiddies!"

"Flurry was eager for me to think his brother had done the job—done it to prove you were the murderer. What if Flurry was prowling after *him*, made it look as if it were all Kevin's doing—the fire and the 'confession'? So we're led to believe it was a desperate attempt by Kevin to throw off our suspicion *he* had killed Mrs. Leeson."

"Such a cat's-cradle of dotty over-subtlety I've never ——"

"Flurry was very pat about the way the fire was started, didn't you notice that?"

"Flurry did not kill his wife. That I know."

"And how do you know it?" Concannon gave me his most disturbing look.

"I just know it."

"He had the biggest motive, and the perfect opportunity."

"I don't care."

"It's a queer thing how loyal you two are to each other."

"You'll be saying next we were in a conspiracy to murder Harriet."

"And I'm not talking about jealousy alone as a motive for him. She was extravagant with money——"

"I never noticed it."

"—and Flurry was nearly broke. D'you know how much money he owes his brother? If Kevin was hanged for the murder, that'd end Flurry's financial troubles."

" But——"

" Kevin has left a legacy to Flurry in his will. He's a rich man. Maire Leeson gets the bulk of the estate."

" So of course Maire has a strong motive too," I said satirically.

" Where there's money, there's always occasion for crime."

After which pious statement, Concannon fell silent. Throughout, he seemed to have been listening for something behind my words, but I was beyond keeping up my guard against him. He had that abstracted, listening look still, though. I felt he was waiting for something.

" You know," I offered presently, " I believe you've been weaving fantasies all this time. Out of the top of your head. Kidding me along, just to pass the time."

Concannon, stirring in his chair, gave me a half smile and opened his mouth to speak. At this instant there was a loud double-explosion somewhere outside. The superintendent and I raced through the door. " Oh God," I thought, " Flurry's shot himself."

When we got to the cobbled yard at the back, Seamus met us, a double-barrelled shotgun in one hand, a large dog fox dangling from the other. The rain had stopped.

" I have him at last. Been stealing hens. He's the bold one—I never knew a fox that tried it on be daylight."

" Lucky you had your gun," said Concannon.

We were hardly in the house again when the telephone rang. I heard Flurry padding out from the fishing room. Then he bawled, " It's for you, Concannon."

I was left alone in the drawing-room. Why it should happen then, I don't know; but I got a fit of the horrors, imagining myself awoken in that little bedroom, a sheet of flame all round me, the bed burning, the tiny window I could not get through, despair and agony, my body curling up in the blaze like a leaf.

When Concannon came in, it was almost as if he was rescuing me from the furnace, the trap. He looked, for him, almost complacent. He rubbed his hands. " I have to be off. You know, Mr. Eyre, you're a terrible stubborn man."

" Am I?"

" Tell me this. What was Harriet Leeson doing, lying in her pelt by the stream if she wasn't awaiting her lover? Sun-bathing? You still say you didn't keep an assignation with her that night?"

I shook my head.

A strange, hypnotic, almost crooning note came into his voice. " You've come clean about everything else. Why are you holding out on me about this? Why are you?"

I stayed silent.

" I'll tell you why, then. You've never forgiven yourself for leaving her there to the mercy of—— You've never forgiven yourself for rejecting her at the last. You never will. You want to make yourself believe it did not happen that way. You never will. You'll bear the scars of her wounds on your heart all your life. I'm sorry for you."

The extraordinary man would have had me broken down in a minute more. But the telephone rang again. " It's for you, Dominic," called Flurry. " Maire wants you."

I was glad to escape Concannon's devastating approach. But Maire's was no less unnerving in its way. She spoke like an automaton. " Dominic, can you come over at once. I'm in great trouble."

" Yes, of course. What's the matter?"

Her control faltered and broke. " They've arrested Kevin."

Chapter 13

Charlottestown had a changed look for me as I drove along the main street and parked my car by Kevin's house—the look of a disaster area, shuttered, silent, stricken. Apart from two tough characters who scrutinised me keenly as I got out of the car, there seemed to be no one about. Surely they've not arrested the whole population? I thought. The atmosphere could not have been more eerie if the plague had descended upon this seedy little township. It was as unnerving in its way as when I had been sent to Coventry at my first school—the sense of total isolation.

It was a relief when Maire opened the door and hurried me into Kevin's study. Three small, freckled faces had stared at me uncomprehendingly from the end of the passage. "Don't hang about, children. For pity's sake, do something! Run out and play: it's fine again."

This in itself was a sufficient contrast from Maire's customary equable manner. She seemed to have gone to pieces: her high colouring looked hectic now, her hair was bedraggled, her eyes watered.

"It's the disgrace," she muttered. "How will the children ever live it down?"

"What's been happening, Maire? I'm entirely in the dark."

"I don't know where to turn," she exclaimed. "If only Father Bresnihan was here."

"Is there nothing I can do?"

"Kathleen says he's expected back this evening. It's terrible—they whisked him away. They wouldn't let me even talk to him first."

" Kevin?"

" Yes." She broke down, sobbing. When she had recovered herself a little, I asked her what Kevin had been charged with.

" I don't *know*," wailed Maire. " I just daren't think."

" Well now, it's not a Police State. He can have his lawyer, can't he? Did you ring the lawyer yet?"

" What'd be the use? The man who took Kevin away told me they were taking him to Dublin."

" Dublin? Why on earth——?"

" I don't *know*!"

After a while, it all came out. Maire had been shopping and then gone for a talk with the schoolmistress. She was just returning to the house when she saw a strange car outside it. The front door opened. Three men appeared with Kevin and bundled him into the car. One of them said, " We're taking your husband to Dublin for questioning. Say good-bye to him. We'll be in touch with you."

" Were they in uniform, these men?"

" They were not."

" And Kevin said nothing to you?"

" No. He hardly seemed to see me. He looked as if the sky had fallen on his head. When I came in, there were two other men opening drawers in his desk here. They've only just left. They pushed me out. I couldn't get a word from them."

" But did none of these men show you a warrant for the arrest?"

" They did not. I was too moithered to think of asking them. And the children were crying."

I thought of Nazi Germany. I thought of the Trouble— the sudden visitation, the man whisked away from his family to a secret tribunal, and maybe never seen again. What proof was there that Kevin's captors had been official police? I did not mention this to Maire. But I asked could I use her telephone. She nodded dumbly. I rang Flurry first: Concannon had left. I tried the Galway station, but a Garda told me the Super was not back yet. Finally, I got on to the Garda at Charlottestown. The voice of the bovine sergeant, who had so notably failed to clear up my own troubles, was not reassuring.

"Mr. Kevin Leeson has been taken away from his house by a body of men. Were they *bona fide?*"

"Don't worry your head about that, Mr. Eyre."

"*I'm* not worrying. It's Mrs. Leeson. She wants to know what it's all about."

"She'd have a right," replied the voice with maddening cosiness. "Time enough, Mr. Eyre. The Super'll be visiting her this evening."

"But for God's sake, man! Mrs. Leeson should be told what her husband's been charged with."

"She will, she will."

"Told *now.*"

"I have my orders."

"But surely—is it the murder?"

I could almost hear the sergeant's brain cumbrously ticking over the telephone line. "What makes you think it'd be the murder?"

"Oh, sod you!" I banged the receiver down. Maire was staring at me in desperate surmise, her green eyes nearly starting from their sockets.

"His lips are sealed. From the way he prevaricated, I got the impression that Kevin has been arrested for murder. Though I don't know why everyone has to make such a mystery about it. I'm sorry, Maire."

She stood up, back to me, her body bowed and rigid, her head leaning against the wall—an immemorial attitude of the woman in shock. After a long while, she turned round. "I was afraid of it. Oh Dominic, I was so afraid of it," she said brokenly, slumping down again into a chair.

I patted her shoulder. I felt dreadfully ill at ease. "Try not to worry, Maire. Try to believe he'll be proved innocent."

"Oh, if only he'd been more open with me! I'd have forgiven him. He kept everything to himself, so I couldn't help him. That woman—she's been the ruin of everything. When I saw her that night——" Maire broke off abruptly.

"*Saw* her?"

She gave me a strange look, half flurried, half sly. "I don't know what you'll think of me. I didn't tell you all the truth about what happened the night she was killed. It doesn't matter, now they've arrested him. Nothing matters."

The proud head lifted to me. The eyes had an inward look. "I told you I wandered about in the demesne. I was miserable—angry with myself that I could go spying after him—it's so humiliating to find you've sunk to that. Well, I *did* see her."

"Yes?"

"I was creeping quietly about. You know that screen of trees on the edge of the demesne, between the rough pasture and the river. I looked out from there. It was dark; but not so dark I couldn't see her lying on the grass by the Lissawn." Her face contorted. "Stretched out naked, sprawling like a whore."

"Yes?"

"And then it—the body—disappeared."

"*Disappeared?*"

"A patch of darkness came between me and it. That's what it seemed like the first moment. The next, I knew it must be a man, in a dark suit. The darkness stayed there a little. I was too far away to hear anything that was said. Then I saw her arms again, coming round the dark figure, as if—as if she was trying to pull it down on to her. I couldn't stand any more. I ran away. Blindly. To get out of the place. I sat down by the track awhile. It was horrible." Maire burst into a storm of sobbing.

"But, Maire," I said presently, "you couldn't recognise this black figure you saw. How could you know it was Kevin?"

"Who else could it be?"

"It could have been me," I managed to get out. "Did you never think it might have been?"

"No. Well, not at the time. I was expecting it to be Kevin, so I assumed—— It wasn't you, was it?"

"No."

"And then Kevin did come home. And he was in a dark suit. And he seemed to be behaving in a very queer way. Irritable, exhausted—I don't know how to put it—he wasn't *with* me. He was like a stranger. So when I heard that Harry——"

"But Maire, if—wouldn't you have seen blood on his clothes?"

She shuddered. "I don't know. I suppose so."

"The police examined them, too."

"I just thought he'd somehow avoided——"

"And you never hinted to him what was in your mind?"

"Oh, I'd never dare. I did ask him, what he'd been doing that evening and why he was so late home. He said about the car running out of petrol. I didn't like to tell him I'd been out looking for him." Maire gave me a little sad ghost of an appealing smile. "I'm afraid you've a lot to forgive me for, Dominic."

"Me? Forgive *you*?"

"If I'd told Mr. Concannon what I've just told you, he'd never have had you under suspicion. You must've been going through a dreadful ordeal. I know you—you were sweet on her," added Maire shyly.

"You've got a good deal more to forgive me for."

"I don't understand."

"Well, you see, I passed on to Concannon what you told me about Kevin's movements that night."

Maire's mouth tightened.

"I know you were talking to me in confidence. But I was in a worse jam myself. In fact, Concannon didn't seem all that interested. But I'm sorry. Truly."

"And I suppose you want me to tell him what *I* was doing—straying about in the demesne?"

Underneath the edge of sarcasm, I seemed to feel a touch of apprehension in her voice.

"No, I said nothing about you, except that you'd bicycled out to meet Kevin, waited at the cross, and then returned home by the same route."

"How can I believe you?" But I detected a note of relief.

"I wouldn't give *you* away. That would have been despicable. But I had no cause to love *Kevin*."

The moment it was out, I realised how Maire could misinterpret that last remark. She gazed at me a moment.

"You mean, you do have cause to like me?" she asked in her most forthright way.

"I—what I mean is you've never done me any harm—you've been awfully kind to me."

Maire averted her eyes. "And Kevin *has* done you harm? How?"

"Well, that boycott. And——"

"And?" she prompted.

I seized the nettle. "I believe he may have had the cottage burnt down. *And* had me dumped on the strand where I nearly drowned."

"You must be mad, Dominic." She sounded genuinely puzzled. "Why on earth should he do that? He liked you."

I replied, as lightly as I could, "You're not the only jealous person in Charlottestown, Maire dear."

"Ah, get on with you!" She gave a tentative laugh.

Then her handsome face clouded again. "I don't know how we can talk like this, with him gone from me. I ought to be ashamed of myself."

"You won't do him any good by moping."

"No, I won't, will I?" she replied in a strangely childish tone. Oh, the docility of women! "But what am I to do, Dominic?"

"Hang on. Survive. It may be all a dreadful mistake. Have a talk with Father Bresnihan when he comes back. Even if the worst happens, you still have the children. And I'll do what I can. One day, when all this is over——"

"Ah, this is disgusting talk," she cried, her mood suddenly changing. She glanced at me suspiciously. "There's some men take advantage of a woman in distress. So they tell me."

"Well, I'm not one of them."

"You're a great comfort to me, my dear. Isn't it strange to be talking with you like this. The first time we met, I thought you were terrible stuck-up."

I knew I was in the danger zone. Maire's conventionality and repressions were beginning to fall off her like clothes— an effect of the ordeal she had gone through these last days. And I was tired, careless, at the end of my tether.

"Maire, did you—do you love Kevin?" It came out before I could stop it.

Her eyes widened.

"*Love* him? But of course, I love him. He's my husband."

I smiled at her.

"You're wicked to tease me like that. I *did* love him. I wanted to do everything for him—die for him, if need be——"

"And be a paragon of pure Irish womanhood. After Father Bresnihan's model. But after a bit you found yourself turned into just another housewife, with a husband who kept all the interesting part of his life locked away from you."

"You're very cynical, Dominic."

"You know it's true."

Her mouth quivered. She gave me a long, probing look. Next moment she had thrown herself at my feet, crying, "Oh, Dominic. I'm so lonely!"

I had not intended this, though I realised I had asked for it. I was lonely too. There was a great hole in my life that begged to be filled up. Maire's face was hot, still damp with tears: her breath was hot on my cheek. I kissed her. For a moment she went rigid in my arms; then her body relaxed, and she startled me with her passion. No, it was not passion, I thought, only a desperate search for oblivion in my arms.

We kissed a while. But, for me, it was no good. Harriet came between me and Maire. She had spoilt me for other women. Two lines of Meredith forced themselves into my head—

> *A kiss is but a kiss now! and no wave*
> *Of a great flood that whirls me to the sea.*

I pushed Maire gently away from me. Her eyes had a blind look.

"I'm sorry, dear, but this won't do. It's all wrong," I said.

"Yes." She was standing over me, flushed, tidying her hair automatically. She had great dignity. "You're unhappy too, aren't you, Dominic?"

It was not till I had started back to Lissawn that the real revulsion came. What had possessed me to behave as I had with Maire? flirting with her, exploiting the disorientation Kevin's absence had caused in her? It was morally squalid. And, for that matter, what had driven Maire to behave so out of character? As soon as I asked myself this, I began wondering what her nature really was. I had had little experience of women before Harriet; and Harriet had given me an advanced course in female strategy. We had played a thrilling game of stratagems with each other—a game so absorbing that it seemed to cover the whole gamut of the sex war. I had never fully trusted Harriet, never quite known where I was with her. How delicious had been the stimulus of thatu ncertainty! And now, Harriet would impose her own pattern upon my relationship with other women.

Maire, who had at first seemed so different—so strait-laced, sexless, forthright, consistent—I was now seeing her as a woman, as the idea of Woman Harriet had planted in me. Was not Maire, too, a mercurial person beneath her habit and training—inconsistent, devious, a bit sly perhaps, even a liar? Manipulating men unconsciously as Harriet had consciously manipulated me?

I began to question the account Maire had just given me of seeing Harriet by the Lissawn that night, seeing the dark figure standing over her, and running away. There was nothing implausible about it. Yet it seemed strange that a jealous woman, who had come out to find her husband in the act, should not have yelled out at him, exposed him there and then, instead of creeping tamely home: or at least, if she were not sure of the figure's identity, gone near enough to confirm it. Would not her rabid jealousy have overcome any puritanical disgust?

Suppose, for argument's sake, Maire had made this story up. What reason would she have to do so *unless the dark figure had been herself*? Maire had clearly been relieved to hear that I had not passed on to Concannon her first story about her movements that night. Then, why did she change it just now? Perhaps, believing I would tell Concannon, to put another nail in her husband's coffin. No, surely her jealousy was not so extreme. It was all too baffling. Anyway, the police had presumably examined her clothes as well as Kevin's, and found no bloodstains on them. And yet again, I could see Maire as a Clytemnestra figure: it was difficult to imagine Kevin as anything more than an Aegisthus.

Then an extremely nasty thought occurred to me. Women, I reflected (meaning Harriet) had an instinctive skill in working on a man's desire by talking about sex. Maire's description of Harriet sprawling naked by the river, of her arms coming up to encircle the dark figure—it made me a participant with her in the sexual scene, a mental voyeur. Was this what, unconsciously, she had been aiming at? And then she had, as they say, thrown herself at my head.

No, no, it was ridiculous fantasy. Maire was merely a distraught woman, compelled to reach out blindly for any sort of comfort. . . .

Flurry and I were quietly soaking in his study when Concannon turned up again, about half past six. I had not been very forthcoming about my talk with Maire, and Flurry was no less taciturn. He greeted the visitor, though, affably enough, sitting him down in the best chair and putting a glass of whiskey in his hand. Concannon looked as if he were suffering from the aftermath of a crisis.

"So you've arrested my brother?" said Flurry without preamble.

"Yes. I'm sorry about it, for your sake."

"Has he confessed?"

"He'll be making a full statement in Dublin to-morrow."

"Do you usually take murderers to Dublin?"

"Kevin Leeson is not charged with murder."

As soon as he said it, I realised how little all this time I had believed that Kevin could do murder. There was a silence.

"Well, I'm glad to hear that," said Flurry at last. Knowing his own plans for dealing with the murderer, I could imagine he was more than glad. I said,

"*Not* the murder? What on earth has he been charged with, then?"

"What you would call treason, Mr. Eyre. Treason."

Flurry sighed heavily. "I was afraid of it. The poor bloody fool. I should have tried to talk him out of it. I blame myself."

"You knew he was mixed up in some political activity?"

"I did not. I guessed he might be. But I thought there was no use talking to him about it. He wouldn't be told by me. How long have you known this?"

"We've had suspicions since early this year, but nothing to go on. Mr. Eyre gave us the first clue."

"Did I indeed? What was that?"

"You remember overhearing the stranger say to Kevin in his study, 'Force is no good at all'?"

"Yes. But——"

"It was the man's pronunciation of Pfaus. Oscar Pfaus is a German-American journalist who came over here in February. He and his masters were the most ignorant eejuts—would you believe it?—Pfaus was sent to contact the I.R.A. through General O'Duffy!"

"Good lord!" I exclaimed. "Like trying to contact Harry Pollitt through Oswald Mosley."

"I wouldn't know about them fellas. Anyway, this Pfaus did in the end get round to Twomey, Russell and a few other I.R.A. extremists."

"The idea being for the I.R.A. to create enough trouble in the North, when Hitler starts his war, to draw a lot of British troops off him?"

"That's roughly it, Mr. Eyre."

"And my brother was mixed up in this nonsense?" asked Flurry.

"Well, he was and he wasn't. He had bigger ideas. The man Mr. Eyre heard talking to him—the Special Branch tracked him down in the end—is a fella called Geogehan. He and your brother are undercover members of an ultra-extremist group of the I.R.A. This group was planning to seize political power, not just to divert some units of the English army."

"It sounds fantastic," I said.

"You'd be surprised what can happen in this country. Kevin Leeson is the new type of Irishman, God help us. An organiser, a businessman—he's interested in power for himself. Travelling around the country, he'd whipped up quite a following, in political and business circles."

"But he'd never win the Army over," said Flurry.

"Armies do what they're told by politicians. Even Irish armies sometimes."

"But you mean he was planning to set up some kind of dictatorship?" I asked.

"Him and Geogehan and a few others. With German help. We've got them all in the bag now. The Special Branch has been following them for the last month or so. It was a tricky business: we didn't want to jump the gun in one place, and alarm the others. We roped them all in, from different parts of the country, at the same hour this morning."

There was a silence. Concannon rubbed his tired eyes with his knuckles.

"So you were right," I said to Flurry. "Those attempts on me were made by your brother to frighten me out of the country and to ensure that I kept silent when I got home."

"Kevin arranged that scare you had on the strand," said Concannon. "Geogehan, Haggerty and another fella carried it out. The burning of your cottage is another matter. Kevin may well have been behind that: we have no proof yet."

"But that was an attempt to kill me, surely, not just to frighten me away?"

"Oh, Kevin was beginning to lose his head by then. I was pushing him hard about the killing of Mrs. Leeson."

"You suspected him of it then?"

"Never a bit. I wanted to break his nerve, so he'd do something foolish over the political conspiracy. And he did."

"How was that?"

"He started telling lies and contradicting himself about that journey down from Galway. We knew he'd gone to Oughterard to consult with one of his associates in the plot —he was being shadowed, but we lost him. You see, he had to conceal the object of his Galway visit: but, when he thought we suspected him of the murder, he was between the devil and the deep blue sea. It was a matter of timing. I won't go into it all now. But he could only throw dust in our eyes about the Galway visit, if he admitted he was in the near vicinity when Mrs. Leeson was killed. Or vice-versa."

"And he'd get off one horn of the dilemma by burning me alive in the cottage and faking my confession?"

"That's about the size of it. He didn't dare betray the political conspiracy. Geogehan's a firebrand and would have cut his throat. Anyway, Kevin got flustered under questioning about the murder: but it drew his attention off the possibility we might be after him for the other reason."

"Things were simpler in my day. We had only the one worry," said Flurry with a touch of sadness. He began to hum "It's the most distressful country "——

I broke in sharply, "So you've not had much chance, with all this excitement, to investigate the murder."

"Time enough, Mr. Eyre, time enough."

"There may be for you; but I've got to get home. I can't sponge on Flurry much longer."

"You're welcome," said Flurry automatically.

"You're going to transfer your war of nerves to us now, are you?"

"Us?" Concannon's heavy eyes turned on me.

"Flurry. Myself. And——" I cut it off.

"And?"

"And anyone else you may suspect."

I could not say Maire's name. I simply could not bring myself to put into words my uneasiness about her. I have enough Irish in me to shrink from the word "informer." I had done enough harm already.

"I've a diver coming from Cork to-morrow," said Concannon.

"Have you now?" Flurry's voice was uninterested, but I felt a new attentiveness in him.

"To find the knife?" I asked.

"There's plenty knives here." Flurry gestured vaguely round the fishing room.

"And here's the ones I took away," said Concannon, unloading his pocket. "They've been tested. Result negative."

"So you'll find the murderer's knife in that deep pool and hang him on the strength of it? Is that your idea?"

"We'll find the knife first, and then go on from there." Concannon gazed fixedly at Flurry. "Of course, it won't have your wife's blood on it still"—the superintendent rapped this out like an accusation; I never liked those calculated brutalities of his—"but I daresay it'll give us all we need." Flurry showing no visible reaction, Concannon added, "Aren't you interested in me finding your wife's murderer?"

"Oh, sure I am." Flurry stabbed one finger in the direction of Concannon's chest. "But let me tell you, boyo— you'll be wasting a man's time leaving him by the Lissawn till your diver comes."

The superintendent was disconcerted. "What are you talking about?"

"You know," growled Flurry. "That pool's eight foot deep now, and the water still rising. I'm no bloody swimmer. If you expect me to plunge in to-night and retrieve the knife and hide it somewhere else, you're an eejut."

Concannon gave a grim smile. "I'll be leaving a man here for all that. I wouldn't like you to drown."

The two men had become antagonists—worthy of each other too—I imagined an invisible salute passing between them. Concannon, I thought, is the sagacious hound, weaving and feinting round the bear—Flurry's small eyes had a wary glint in them, his huge paw-like hands hung down relaxed. I felt suddenly suffocated by the knowledge that in this duel it was Concannon who would surely win.

"If you think Flurry could have killed Harriet, you'll be making the most unforgiveable mistake in your life."

"Thanks for the unsolicited tribute, me boy."

"It's very touching," said Concannon. "And Flurry will say just the same for you, no doubt."

"I will. And let me tell you this, Concannon. If ever I swing for anyone, it'll not be Harriet. Will you take a bet on it?"

The Superintendent shook his head, with an appraising look at Flurry. They seemed to be trying to outstare each other, like children. Then Concannon said a brusque farewell.

Flurry watched him through the window as he went to the car. "Look there, Dominic. Just as I thought. He has a fella with him; and the poor sod'll have to stay up all night watching for me to plunge into the Lissawn. It's a great shame. We'd best bring out a bed for him."

I was in no condition to enter into Flurry's high spirits.

"C'mon. Drink up. That's better. I hope you don't walk in your sleep."

" Why——?"

" You're a great swimmer, aren't you? Don't go taking a fancy to walking in your sleep and diving into the river. It'd look bad.''

For a long time that night I could not get to sleep. It was still only the fifth night since Harriet's death, but that seemed to have taken place in another life of mine, ages back. Murders are seldom solved in a week, I imagine; yet I felt an unaccountable impatience with Concannon. I wanted to be put out of my misery and uncertainty. I could understand the murderer's state of mind, which leads him consciously or unconsciously to break the log-jam in it by giving himself up, or giving himself away.

Once again I was possessed by the terror lest I had killed Harriet myself in some paranoiac frenzy. I was the highest up on my own short list of suspects: perhaps Concannon, a patient man, was waiting for me to betray myself. Kevin was now struck off the list. There only remained Flurry, Maire, me, and a shadowy X—the wandering man Maire had seen as she bicycled home, who then appeared to have vanished off the face of the earth.

I was living now in a total unreality, as if in a vacuum, which made the happy times with Harriet equally unreal. It seemed incredible that I should have treated Flurry all those weeks in so despicable a way: it was not in my character, surely; but it had happened—a game I had played, as I felt now, with dream figures—with Harriet, who had turned me into a dream figure. Father Bresnihan had woken me out of the dream. Or was that a pretentious interpretation? Was it not simply that I had grown tired of Harriet?

But the dream-feeling obsessed me, as Harriet had done. If now our whole life together had this quality of dream, it seemed more than likely that I had put an end to hers in some sleep of consciousness.

That dark figure which, Maire said, had blotted out Harriet's white body—was it X or Flurry, or me; or Maire herself? I fought against the idea that it was any of the last three. Perhaps least of all did I want it to be Flurry, for I had him so desperately on my conscience. Yet it was he, I judged, whom Concannon now had his mind set on.

It occurred to me at this moment that I had never tried to put myself in Harriet's place. She is lying on the grass by the river, naked and rather tipsy. I have just left her, having said we must never again be lovers—having refused to make love with her a last time. She is angry, defeated, weeping. Would she not have soon put on her night-dress and hurried back to the house?

I myself had returned to the cottage and not gone to sleep immediately. Even if my mind had split, and I'd returned to kill her, she would surely not have been there still when I returned.

Oh yes, she might have gone to sleep, worn out with emotional stress.

But, if Maire's story was true, Harriet had been sufficiently awake to put her arms round the dark figure. If this figure was a strange man, our X, she would not do so: she would yell out and try to run away. If it was Maire herself, armed with a knife, Harriet would not have gone on lying there, like a lamb for the slaughter.

Flurry then? She opens her eyes and sees her husband standing before her. She would not inevitably cry out or run away. "What are you doing here?" he asks. "I was so hot. I wandered out, and went to sleep. "Well, get up. You'll catch your death of cold out here." "Come, Flurry ——" she raises her arms to pull him down or for him to pull her up: she could always twist him round her finger, she thinks.

But there, my fantasy fell to pieces. Why should Flurry pull out a knife? Why, if he did, hadn't Maire heard her screaming? Harriet would not have been an easy victim: she was certainly no death-wish girl. If Maire had waited a minute longer, she would have seen the struggle and its end.

But was there a struggle, apart from the usual sex-gymnastics? . . . The child she was carrying. Suppose that Flurry rejected her advances or was incapable of responding to them. I could just (but only just) imagine Harriet, in a fury of frustration, taunting him with this child—saying, or hinting, that it was not his. Flurry himself had told me what store he set on having a child by her: he never for a moment seemed to have doubted it was his. The shock of learning it was not would have sent him off his head. Her manner of death—all those little wounds, looked like the work of a madman, of someone striking out blindly again and again in a frenzy, as if the body lying there had become an object of extreme repulsion, a false and loathsome succubus.

The next morning would show how close I had come to the truth—and how remote from it I had been too.

Chapter 14

Because I had slept so little that night, only dropping off at dawn, I did not awake till half nine. There were faint voices from below, and presently I heard the front door opened and footsteps receding through the garden.

When I got downstairs, I found Concannon's man chatting with Seamus over breakfast.

"Hallo," I said to him. "I thought you were supposed to see none of us jumped in the river."

He grinned sheepishly. "Ah, Mr. Flurry'll be safe enough with the Father."

"Father Bresnihan's after arriving," Seamus explained. "Flurry took him out fishing. He looks as if he'd seen a ghost. Maybe the fresh air will recover him."

I ate the boiled egg Seamus had waiting for me in a cosy, and some soda bread.

"When will you be relieved?" I asked the young Garda.

"At midday, please God. Have you any more eggs, Seamus? There's a powerful hunger on me still."

"What's Father Bresnihan want so early?"

"I didn't hear," said Seamus indifferently. "I was too busy cooking for this fella. Why the hell don't you go and guard something, Rory?"

"And I destroyed with midges and the want of sleep? Have you no mercy at all?"

"Want of sleep, is it? Sure, I wager you'd not an eye open all night."

"I did so," exclaimed the Garda indignantly.

"And how many ghosts did *you* see?"

"Never a one. Only the water, and it boiling up against

the great rocks all night. There's a powerful flood in it off the mountains. Mr. Flurry'll not be catching anything this morning."

"Mr. Flurry'ld draw a fish out of the river of hell, if he had a mind to it. Anyway, it's overcast and there's no wind."

In a few minutes I walked out into the demesne, picking up Flurry's old field-glasses on the way. It was one of those morbid mornings when everything seems shut-in, silent, inanimate—a cataleptic trance of nature. Cattle stood about, their heads bowed, stupidly regarding the grass in front of them as if it were an insoluble problem. The birds might have gone into retreat: not a cheep or a flutter from the trees. The only sound was the faint roaring of the Lissawn, away to my left, amplified in the windless air, and presently the noise of a car driving up the avenue.

It was Kevin's. I intercepted it, and Maire leant out of the driver's window.

"Is the Father here?"

"Yes, Flurry's just taken him out by the river."

"I rang him last night, but Kathleen said he was too tired to see anyone. And when I rang again after breakfast, she told me he was visiting over here."

"Well, there's no hurry, is there? Get out, and we'll go and find him."

"I must talk to him about Kevin," said Maire, rather wildly. "I have a terrible load on my mind, Dominic."

She drove her car on to the grass beside the avenue, hitting its front bumper against an ash tree, and got out. "I don't seem able to do anything right nowadays," she muttered, almost in tears. Her eyes were downcast; what had happened yesterday between her and me might never have happened. The proud face looked frozen.

A vague idea came into my mind. I would take Maire to the place, overlooking the green spit by the Lissawn, from

which that night she had seen Harriet and the murderer—
or had seen Harriet and murdered her. I would make her
envisage the scene again. Perhaps that would cause her to
betray herself. As we walked silently over the grass, I tried
to imagine myself pouncing hard on Maire with brutal
questions, like a policeman, though what questions I could
ask her were not in the least clear to me. I felt myself on
the edge of some revelation, nervous and fatalistic.

"I haven't had a word yet from the superintendent," she
said out of the silence.

"They took Kevin on some political charge," I replied
uncomfortably. "Not the murder."

"Oh? I don't understand this at all. *Political?*" But
Maire had no time to ask the questions that must have been
crowding to her tongue; for we had arrived at the screen of
trees, and were met by a sight so bizarre that for a moment
I really believed I had gone mad.

Fifty yards away, his back to us, Flurry stood at the
water's edge holding a rod. The river hurried and foamed
past him. And in the middle of it a black-clad figure
floundered, then disappeared from view into the deep pool,
and presently emerged again, holding something up in its
right hand. I focused my glasses on it. The figure was
Father Bresnihan's, water streaming down his distraught
face. Maire gave a cry and made to run forward, but I
clamped a hand on her wrist.

What had led up to this weird scene I can only reconstruct
from Flurry Leeson's statement, which Concannon gave me
the gist of next day.

Shortly before I came down to breakfast, Father Bresnihan had turned up. He told Flurry he must have a talk with
him at once, privately. Flurry was just ready to go out
and thrash the river, so he asked the Father to accompany
him.

"You've heard my brother has been arrested?"

"Kathleen told me of it."

"The poor silly eejut—he over-reached himself. Politics are the ruin of this country. You're not looking too well yourself, Father. That retreat doesn't seem to have done you any good. You look like death warmed up, saving your presence."

Father Bresnihan made no reply. When they reached the green spit, he stopped.

"Well, Father," said Flurry good-humouredly, "have you come to hear my confession?"

"That is not a subject I like to hear jokes made about," replied Father Bresnihan automatically.

"Well then, what do you want of me?"

The Father turned his eyes full upon his companion. They flared up from the extinguished face. "I have come to make a confession to you, Flurry. It was I who killed your wife."

"You?—ah now, Father, you're not well. You don't know what you're saying."

"I tell you, I killed your wife. You must believe me."

"Sure you'd never do a thing like that. Of course I don't believe you." Embarrassed, Flurry fiddled with his fishing gear.

"Leave that alone and listen to me," ordered the priest.

"Be easy. I'll get the doctor out. He'll put you right in no time."

"Nothing will ever put me right!" It was like a cry from a damned soul. "God will not forgive me. How can I ask you to? All I want is for you to understand me—my actions. Then I shall give myself up."

"Very well," Flurry answered, in the tone of one humouring a lunatic. "You killed Harriet. How did it come about?"

He sat down on the grass beside Father Bresnihan, who started to tell his story, trying to control his twitching face.

Sometimes the Father's words became a muttering gabble, so that Flurry could hardly make out what he was saying; at others, the beautiful voice slowed and cleared, as if he must convince Flurry at all costs.

"When I left you that night—you remember?—I thought I'd take the short cut along the river here. I was tired. I needed some air. I'd just got to this spot—it *was* here, wasn't it?" Father Bresnihan said, as if he'd only just awoken to the fact. "I came on your wife, lying on the grass. Naked. Shameless. I stood over her, to rebuke her. It was my duty to do so. My duty, you understand?"

"Of course it was," said Flurry, humouring him still. "You can't have naked women lying about all over your parish."

"And it was your duty, as I'd told you half an hour before, to keep your wife in order." Father Bresnihan passed his hand over his face, as if brushing away cobwebs. "The woman was drunk and insolent. Then she tried to clasp me round the knees. I thought at first it was a gesture of supplication. I was wrong. She she she was attempting to seduce me."

The Father was now talking to himself—Flurry might not have been there at all. "She disgusted me. The smell of drink on her. The smell of her body."

"A powerful ordeal for you, Father."

"She would not let go of me. She began a tirade against me. She hissed at me like a serpent. She was in a fury because I had persuaded Dominic Eyre of his evil ways, and he had promised me never again to indulge himself in acts of immorality with her. I told her she was living in mortal sin. It was my duty, though she did not belong to our faith. I told her she was a whore, she would burn with the damned if she'd not change her ways."

"Strong words, Father."

"She mocked at me—told me I was no man, only a

eunuch, a eunuch. I should have left her then." Father Bresnihan gave Flurry a wild look. He shuddered. "But she was terrible strong. She dragged me down to her. I can see now she was set on taking revenge: she wanted to destroy my soul. The flesh. The sweating of flesh. Horrible. The woman was like a mad animal, swarming over me, her hand seeking to expose me. I could not break away from her. She had the strength of the Devil."

The priest broke off, wiping the spittle from his mouth. "I'll not deny you, Flurry, I was tempted," he went on in a different voice. "Sore tempted. I prayed to be delivered from sin. She was laughing. What a triumph for her, to ruin a priest! Now it was my own body, my sinful flesh I had to fight against as well as hers. The place stank with lust. I managed to pull out my penknife and open it. I was frantic. It seemed like driving a knife into my own corrupted flesh. She fell away from me. I had saved myself."

There was a long silence. Father Bresnihan was shivering like a terrified horse.

"I see. And what did you do next?" asked Flurry.

"I had a fearful revulsion. I threw away the knife—the blade flashed in a bit of moonlight—I saw it fall into the deep pool yonder."

"And then?"

"I ran away. I staggered home. There was not a soul in the street to see me. I thought, one place on the track, I heard a bicycle behind me; but it never passed me. It must have been a delusion." Father Bresnihan's sunken eyes regarded Flurry desperately. "I said once, in this house, that murder cannot be condoned—it can only be forgiven. I was wrong. I do not expect you to forgive me. All I want is you should understand why I did it. I have written to the Bishop: now I shall go and give myself up."

"Understand you, Father? Sure I don't even believe you

—not one word of it. You've had a nervous breakdown. You're not yourself at all."

"But I——"

"You were always terrible down on the sins of the flesh. Now they've had their revenge on you. You've imagined the whole thing."

"I wish that was true, Flurry. But it's not."

"Where's the blood then?"

"The blood——?"

"I burnt them in the incinerator when I got back to the presbytery. Kathleen doesn't sleep in. I had the whole night. I soaked them in petrol first. The police would never come looking for a murderer in a priest's house, anyway."

Flurry gazed at him silently.

"And *you* cannot believe a priest would do such a thing, Flurry. We're men, like you, and sometimes our discipline goes."

"You killed Harry because you were frightened of her—of what she was trying to do to you? Degrading you? Is that it?"

"She'd have destroyed my vocation and been the ruin of my soul. Can't you see that?"

"So you killed her in self-defence? Her and my unborn child?"

"Yes," said the Father, almost eagerly, "you could put it that way."

"And then you went into retreat?"

"I was not running away, Flurry. I had to make my peace with God, before I gave myself up."

"And did you succeed?"

Father Bresnihan stared out at the foaming river. "No," he said at last. "God turned his face from me."

Flurry lifted the rod from the grass beside him. "Well,

Father, this is a queer tale. You'll not get anyone to believe it."

"But *you* believe it?" the priest implored.

"I do not. You're overwrought. You need a good long rest."

"But it is true! I tell you, it's true!"

"Prove it then."

"Prove it? But how——?"

"You say you threw your knife into the river. Was that the one with your initials on it?"

"Yes."

"Fetch out that knife, and I'll believe you."

Father Bresnihan stared at him. Did he have any notion, in his disordered brain, of what was happening to him? or why he had been so determined to convince Flurry that his fantastic tale was true? We shall never know.

For myself, I still have the greatest admiration for him. He was a strong character, intelligent, brave and honourable, and I have no doubt a most conscientious priest. Although his silence had put me into a week of misery, wondering if I myself had killed Harriet, knowing myself suspected of it, I could never hold this against him. And I have long forgiven him the killing of Harriet. The extreme loathing, the insidious upsurge of lust which made that loathing even more lurid, because now it was turned upon himself—how could any man have dealt with them? Father Bresnihan remains a tragic figure for me; and tragedy comes, as the Greeks believed, from a fatal flaw.

Bresnihan, in his ignorance and contempt of sex, had all his life defied the most merciless of the gods, Aphrodite. It was she who in a few minutes turned on him and destroyed him.

Perhaps, too, he could be convicted of the sin of pride—an overweening confidence that he would always be armoured against the Aphrodite in woman. I don't know. Harriet never disgusted me; but I can imagine her driving me to a crisis when I would have to draw a knife on her—to hack myself free from those liana-like arms.

At what point Flurry became certain that the Father was telling him the truth, we cannot know. It may have been some while before he challenged him to find the knife. Flurry, after Harriet's death, had turned into a man with but one purpose in his head. I suppose you could say he too, like all monomaniacs, was insane. He was a simple-minded man—half a peasant in his values, a guerrilla by training; amazingly generous when generosity could least be expected --to me; but beneath all this a crafty and ruthless man, to whom an enemy, a man who had destroyed what was nearest to him, was quite simply a life he must take in retribution, and no argument about it.

So, when I saw the last act of the tragedy playing itself before my eyes, I stood as helpless as a Greek chorus, first in a bewildered lack of comprehension, then frozen into immobility.

"Fetch out that knife and I'll believe you," Flurry had said.

And at once Father Bresnihan plunged into the river. The force of the current, the uneven river-bed, caused him to stumble several times. But he forged his way towards the pool, and began clumsily diving into it. Flurry told Concannon that the priest dived in time and again, only to surface empty-handed. It must have been a pitiable sight— the desperate face, the fingers clawing at the rock to prevent him being swept downstream.

It was then that Maire and I arrived. The man in the water held up something, with a cry of triumph as if it had been a pearl. I focused the glasses on him, and saw what it was.

"Wedged in a rock," I could just hear Father Bresnihan shouting.

But why on earth had Flurry sent him out to retrieve it? Then the Father lost his footing again and disappeared, to emerge a little farther downstream, swimming clumsily.

Maire was giving little sobs beside me. I turned the glasses on Flurry, who stood like a boulder at the water's edge. As I did so, he made a cast. I followed the fly, which alighted with the most perfect accuracy a foot or two upstream from Bresnihan's head and a little beyond it.

I could hear Flurry reeling in. I saw the flick of the wrists as he struck. Bresnihan clapped a hand to his ear, as if he had been stung by a hornet, and in doing so went under the water again. When he emerged, there was blood flowing from his ear: he had been hooked in the cartilage of it.

"What in the name of goodness is Flurry doing?" muttered Maire. "That's no way to rescue a man."

What Flurry was doing was slowly to reel in the line, playing his fish, dragging the Father always nearer the bank. He was in the shallows now and could easily have stood up and scrambled the rest of the way, but for Flurry, who kept the line tense, so Bresnihan must either have half his ear torn off or crawl along the river-bed obedient to the line's tug.

It was not till hours after that I realised he could have cut it with the knife he still held in his hand.

Flurry's face was utterly expressionless—only a little pouting of the lips as he judged the strain his line would bear. He looked so ordinary, it made the whole scene still more enigmatic and bizarre. I was so dazed that I could not begin to find a reason for the spectacle Flurry and Father Bresnihan were enacting.

And then the moment of truth was here. The Father, who had indeed been led like a lamb to the slaughter, knelt up on the strip of shingle between the grass and the Lissawn. He could have cut the line, but he did not. I saw Flurry's hand reach down to the grass beside him. I saw the Father hold out the knife to him. I saw him gaze fearlessly at Flurry, and his lips moving. Flurry told Concannon afterwards that Father Bresnihan's last words were, "No, Flurry. Don't take murder on your soul, my son."

But Flurry's right arm rose up, with the gaff in his hand. Maire and I, released from our trance, yelled out and leaped forward. But the gaff struck with murderous violence against the neck of the kneeling man.

EPILOGUE

Epilogue

As the late Dominic Eyre's literary executor, it behoves me to add a few words to this very strange, and for him untypical, story. He himself wrote at the beginning of it, " I do not know if I shall ever bring myself to publish it." After his sudden death a couple of months ago, going through his effects, I came upon the MS, and the decision devolved upon me.

It was a difficult one for two reasons. First, the novel is out of key with his other published works. They are, to the layman's eye, often satirical, somewhat dry in places, but witty and beautifully written, with an air of complete self-possession. *The Private Wound*, on the contrary, is a kind of romantic melodrama (on the title page *Take her up tenderly* has been crossed out and the present title substituted). What Dominic's faithful public will make of it, I cannot imagine: but his publisher, though sharing my doubts, felt it should be given to the world. My second reason for hesitation I shall come to later.

I have often wondered whether this novel (" I dislike confessional writing," he says) was prompted by some intuition of his approaching death. It is true that in one sense he did not need this sort of confession: he had been received into the Catholic Church not long after the last war. But, if the events in the book are at all autobiographical, Dominic might well have come to think that they needed fuller treatment than could be given under the seal of the confessional.

The title he finally chose suggests a course of events which was highly personal and for some reason or other had long been preying upon his mind.

But first I should say something about Dominic himself. We first met in 1940 at an O.C.T.U., and as fellow Anglo-Irishmen struck up a friendship. We were posted to the same unit, and fought side by side in the Western Desert, where he got the M.C.

Like every front-line soldier, he was frequently scared stiff: like every good soldier, he controlled his fear and used it to sharpen his edge in action. He struck me as essentially a cold, or at least a cautious and circumspect man; but he could break out occasionally into a wild, irresponsible mood which made the rest of us, his juniors in age, seem positively stodgy. This combination of traits turned him, as a soldier, into a real professional: he planned with extreme care, then carried out his plans with an almost manic recklessness. At that time, few of us knew that he wrote books: he never spoke of them: the only sign he gave was that writer's abstractedness, the feeling you got from him that now and then he had moved miles away from you into some desert of his own. But he was always polite, unobtrusive, almost self-deprecating.

It was this detachment, together with the outbursts of gaiety and the hard core they felt in him, which won the respect of his men.

Presently he and I transferred to the Long Range Desert Group. Here he was in his element, swanning around in armoured cars, no longer under any obligation to the regimental frame of mind. However, after an extremely successful attack on an airfield eighty miles behind the enemy's lines, we were finally caught out by Rommel's boys and—the few of us who survived—put in the bag.

For a short while we were in the same German hospital, then in the same prisoner-of-war camp. Dominic was not one of those always planning an escape. " Now I can get on with my work," he said to me; and one saw him scribbling away on any piece of paper he could get hold of. He adapted well to the tedious stalag life: but he used to have nightmares, in one of which I heard him muttering over and over a name that sounded like "Harry." When I taxed him with it next morning he went so cold on me that I wondered if I had not unveiled some homosexual secret.

I was transferred to another stalag, and I did not meet Dominic again till after the war. By this time, I had joined my father's firm of solicitors. I met Dominic by chance in my club, where he was a fellow member's guest—he was never a one to go to those Eighth-Army reunion jamborees. He looked well. That curious impression of stillness, of inward-looking, of being separated from other human beings by some invisible barrier, which I am told ex-prisoners of war give, with him was indistinguishable from the writer's mien of abstraction.

Learning that I was in a law firm, he asked if I would act for him in a small piece of litigation he was threatened with. We won the case for him, and some months later he appointed me his executor. By this time, his mother was dead: he had no close relatives: apart from a few minor bequests, the will I drew up for him divided his property between certain Roman Catholic charities in Ireland and a fund for the relief of indigent authors.

I assumed he would marry before long, and the will be altered. He was a personable man, a little below medium height, with the air of mystery which, I am told, women find attractive. He had, to my knowledge, a number of affairs with women; but he never married. His mistresses—I only met one of them—were by all accounts beautiful, dashing and mondaine women, who nevertheless failed to draw him the long step from the bed to the altar.

I was never thoroughly intimate with Dominic. One of our mutual friends described him to me as "a haunted man." I confess I could never see it myself—except in so far as every novelist is haunted by the characters of the book he is momently writing. I asked him once what had led him into the Catholic Church; he said something about a priest he had met before the war and greatly respected. How he reconciled his love-affairs with his church was a matter between him and his confessor. Certainly, during our many conversations, he never mentioned a visit to Ireland in 1939.

And this brings me to my second problem. When I first read the MS., I naturally had inquiries made in the West of Ireland. I did not expect to find a small place called Charlottestown—like most professional writers, Dominic kept a wary eye open to the dangers of libel. Nor, in the district where he set the novel—it would seem to be the north-western end of Co. Clare, but Dominic had given fictional names to all the natural features he mentioned—was there any evidence for the existence of the characters who appear in it. He would not, of course, have used the names of real people; and it could be imagined that, in any case, such an appalling scandal, involving a parish priest, would be hushed up. But in the newspapers of that time we found no mention of a sensational crime of violence or a political trial involving persons in Co. Clare.

So Dominic made the whole thing up? I found this difficult to swallow, for the reasons I have already given. Why, at his time of life, should Dominic have written a novel of romantic melodrama, so out of character with all his previous books, unless some non-literary motive was at work in him? And how to account for the raw experience the book seems to embody—the sense I got when first I read the MS., that something like this must really have happened to him?

I do not pretend to understand the mysteries of the craft. I remember Dominic once saying to me that there is no such thing as a purely fictional character: every character in a novel has grown from the seed of some real person—a person the author has met, if only for a few moments, in "real life," or one whom he has built up from some personality in himself. "We are all teeming with unborn children," he said—"possible selves we have never brought to life."

So it may well be, I reason, that although the events of the book are fictional, they represent some conflict, some authentic experience, which Dominic underwent in his thirties. The central relationship, between him and the woman he calls Harriet Leeson, may have developed in another part of Ireland, in England, or somewhere abroad for that matter. He would want to "distance" himself from the experience, in place as well as time. Whatever the experience had been, he never gave me or any of our mutual friends the least inkling of it.

I would have been content to leave it at that—a fiction lightly based on a long-buried fact—but for two things.

A week ago, I happened to read a book by Timothy Coogan entitled *Ireland since the Rising*. On pp. 270-1 of this admirable study in recent Irish history, I read that "a German-American journalist called Oscar Pfaus was sent to Ireland on February 3rd, 1939, to make contact with the I.R.A.—through General O'Duffy!" The book was published *after* Dominic's death.

Well, I suppose Dominic *might* have heard about this Pfaus from some other source: he visited Ireland occasionally, though he seemed to me quite uninterested in the country's politics.

But then, going through his effects, I had found something the significance of which I had no means of grasping till later I read the MS. of *The Private Wound*. Tucked away on the shelf above Dominic's suits in his wardrobe, I found a cap, faded cherry-red in colour. A kind of jockey cap.

Harman Tooley, 1967

THE PERENNIAL LIBRARY MYSTERY SERIES

E. C. Bentley

TRENT'S LAST CASE
"One of the three best detective stories ever written."
—Agatha Christie

TRENT'S OWN CASE
"I won't waste time saying that the plot is sound and the detection satisfying. Trent has not altered a scrap and reappears with all his old humor and charm."
—Dorothy L. Sayers

Gavin Black

A DRAGON FOR CHRISTMAS
"Potent excitement!"
—New York Herald Tribune

THE EYES AROUND ME
"I stayed up until all hours last night reading The Eyes Around Me, which is something I do not do very often, but I was so intrigued by the ingeniousness of Mr. Black's plotting and the witty way in which he spins his mystery. I can only say that I enjoyed the book enormously."
—F. van Wyck Mason

YOU WANT TO DIE, JOHNNY?
"Gavin Black doesn't just develop a pressure plot in suspense, he adds uninfected wit, character, charm, and sharp knowledge of the Far East to make rereading as keen as the first race-through." —Book Week

Nicholas Blake

THE BEAST MUST DIE
"It remains one more proof that in the hands of a really first-class writer the detective novel can safely challenge comparison with any other variety of fiction."
—The Manchester Guardian

THE CORPSE IN THE SNOWMAN
"If there is a distinction between the novel and the detective story (which we do not admit), then this book deserves a high place in both categories."
—The New York Times

THE DREADFUL HOLLOW
"Pace unhurried, characters excellent, reasoning solid."
—San Francisco Chronicle

END OF CHAPTER
". . . admirably solid . . . an adroit formal detective puzzle backed up by firm characterization and a knowing picture of London publishing."
—The New York Times

HEAD OF A TRAVELER
"Another grade A detective story of the right old jigsaw persuasion."
—New York Herald Tribune Book Review

MINUTE FOR MURDER
"An outstanding mystery novel. Mr. Blake's writing is a delight in itself."
—The New York Times

THE MORNING AFTER DEATH
"One of Blake's best."
—Rex Warner

A PENKNIFE IN MY HEART
"Style brilliant . . . and suspenseful."
—San Francisco Chronicle

THE PRIVATE WOUND
[Blake's] best novel in a dozen years . . . . An intensely penetrating study of sexual passion . . . . A powerful story of murder and its aftermath."
—Anthony Boucher, *The New York Times*

A QUESTION OF PROOF
"The characters in this story are unusually well drawn, and the suspense is well sustained."
—The New York Times

THE SAD VARIETY
"It is a stunner. I read it instead of eating, instead of sleeping."
—Dorothy Salisbury Davis

THE SMILER WITH THE KNIFE
"An extraordinarily well written and entertaining thriller."
—Saturday Review of Literature

THOU SHELL OF DEATH
"It has all the virtues of culture, intelligence and sensibility that the most exacting connoisseur could ask of detective fiction."
—The Times [London] *Literary Supplement*

THE WHISPER IN THE GLOOM
"One of the most entertaining suspense-pursuit novels in many seasons."
—The New York Times

Nicolas Blake (cont'd)

THE WIDOW'S CRUISE

"A stirring suspense. . . . The thrilling tale leaves nothing to be desired."
—*Springfield Republican*

THE WORM OF DEATH

"It [The Worm of Death] is one of Blake's very best—and his best is better than almost anyone's." —Louis Untermeyer

George Harmon Coxe

MURDER WITH PICTURES

"[Coxe] has hit the bull's-eye with his first shot."
—*The New York Times*

Edmund Crispin

BURIED FOR PLEASURE

"Absolute and unalloyed delight."
—Anthony Boucher, *The New York Times*

Kenneth Fearing

THE BIG CLOCK

"It will be some time before chill-hungry clients meet again so rare a compound of irony, satire, and icy-fingered narrative. *The Big Clock* is . . . a psychothriller you won't put down." —*Weekly Book Review*

Andrew Garve

THE ASHES OF LODA

"Garve . . . embellishes a fine fast adventure story with a more credible picture of the U.S.S.R. than is offered in most thrillers."
—*The New York Times Book Review*

THE CUCKOO LINE AFFAIR

". . . an agreeable and ingenious piece of work." —*The New Yorker*

A HERO FOR LEANDA

"One can trust Mr. Garve to put a fresh twist to any situation, and the ending is really a lovely surprise." —*The Manchester Guardian*

MURDER THROUGH THE LOOKING GLASS

". . . refreshingly out-of-the-way and enjoyable . . . highly recommended to all comers." —*Saturday Review*

NO TEARS FOR HILDA

"It starts fine and finishes finer. I got behind on breathing watching Max get not only his man but his woman, too." —Rex Stout

THE RIDDLE OF SAMSON

"The story is an excellent one, the people are quite likable, and the writing is superior." —*Springfield Republican*

Michael Gilbert

BLOOD AND JUDGMENT

"Gilbert readers need scarcely be told that the characters all come alive at first sight, and that his surpassing talent for narration enhances any plot. . . . Don't miss." —*San Francisco Chronicle*

THE BODY OF A GIRL

"Does what a good mystery should do: open up into all kinds of ramifications, with untold menace behind the action. At the end, there is a bang-up climax, and it is a pleasure to see how skilfully Gilbert wraps everything up." —*The New York Times Book Review*

THE DANGER WITHIN

"Michael Gilbert has nicely combined some elements of the straight detective story with plenty of action, suspense, and adventure, to produce a superior thriller." —*Saturday Review*

DEATH HAS DEEP ROOTS

"Trial scenes superb; prowl along Loire vivid chase stuff; funny in right places; a fine performance throughout." —*Saturday Review*

FEAR TO TREAD

"Merits serious consideration as a work of art."
—*The New York Times*

C. W. Grafton

BEYOND A REASONABLE DOUBT

"A very ingenious tale of murder . . . a brilliant and gripping narrative."
—Jacques Barzun and Wendell Hertig Taylor

Edward Grierson

THE SECOND MAN

"One of the best trial-testimony books to have come along in quite a while." —*The New Yorker*

Cyril Hare

AN ENGLISH MURDER
"By a long shot, the best crime story I have read for a long time. Everything is traditional, but originality does not suffer. The setting is perfect. Full marks to Mr. Hare."   —*Irish Press*

TRAGEDY AT LAW
"An extremely urbane and well-written detective story."
                                                —*The New York Times*

UNTIMELY DEATH
"The English detective story at its quiet best, meticulously underplayed, rich in perceivings of the droll human animal and ready at the last with a neat surprise which has been there all the while had we but wits to see it."   —*New York Herald Tribune Book Review*

WHEN THE WIND BLOWS
"The best, unquestionably, of all the Hare stories, and a masterpiece by any standards."
  —Jacques Barzun and Wendell Hertig Taylor, *A Catalogue of Crime*

WITH A BARE BODKIN
"One of the best detective stories published for a long time."
                                                    —*The Spectator*

Matthew Head

THE CABINDA AFFAIR (*available 6/81*)
"An absorbing whodunit and a distinguished novel of atmosphere."
                        —Anthony Boucher, *The New York Times*

MURDER AT THE FLEA CLUB (*available 6/81*)
"The true delight is in Head's style, its limpid ease combined with humor and an awesome precision of phrase."   —*San Francisco Chronicle*

M. V. Heberden

ENGAGED TO MURDER
"Smooth plotting."   —*The New York Times*

James Hilton

WAS IT MURDER?
"The story is well planned and well written."
                                                —*The New York Times*

Elspeth Huxley

THE AFRICAN POISON MURDERS (*available 5/81*)
"Obscure venom, manical mutilations, deadly bush fire, thrilling climax compose major opus.... Top-flight."
—*Saturday Review of Literature*

Francis Iles

BEFORE THE FACT
"Not many 'serious' novelists have produced character studies to compare with Iles's internally terrifying portrait of the murderer in *Before the Fact,* his masterpiece and a work truly deserving the appellation of unique and beyond price." —Howard Haycraft

MALICE AFORETHOUGHT
"It is a long time since I have read anything so good as *Malice Aforethought,* with its cynical humour, acute criminology, plausible detail and rapid movement. It makes you hug yourself with pleasure."
—H. C. Harwood, *Saturday Review*

Lange Lewis

THE BIRTHDAY MURDER
"Almost perfect in its playlike purity and delightful prose."
—Jacques Barzun and Wendell Hertig Taylor

Arthur Maling

LUCKY DEVIL
"The plot unravels at a fast clip, the writing is breezy and Maling's approach is as fresh as today's stockmarket quotes."
—*Louisville Courier Journal*

RIPOFF
"A swiftly paced story of today's big business is larded with intrigue as a Ralph Nader-type investigates an insurance scandal and is soon on the run from a hired gun and his brother. . . . Engrossing and credible."
—*Booklist*

SCHROEDER'S GAME
"As the title indicates, this Schroeder is up to something, and the unravelling of his game is a diverting and sufficiently blood-soaked entertainment." —*The New Yorker*

Thomas Sterling

THE EVIL OF THE DAY

"Prose as witty and subtle as it is sharp and clear. . .characters unconventionally conceived and richly bodied forth . . . . In short, a novel to be treasured." —Anthony Boucher, *The New York Times*

Julian Symons

THE BELTING INHERITANCE

"A superb whodunit in the best tradition of the detective story." —August Derleth, *Madison Capital Times*

BLAND BEGINNING

"Mr. Symons displays a deft storytelling skill, a quiet and literate wit, a nice feeling for character, and detectival ingenuity of a high order." —Anthony Boucher, *The New York Times*

BOGUE'S FORTUNE

"There's a touch of the old sardonic humour, and more than a touch of style." —*The Spectator*

THE BROKEN PENNY

"The most exciting, astonishing and believable spy story to appear in years. —Anthony Boucher, *The New York Times Book Review*

THE COLOR OF MURDER

"A singularly unostentatious and memorably brilliant detective story." —*New York Herald Tribune Book Review*

THE 31ST OF FEBRUARY

"Nobody has painted a more gruesome picture of the advertising business since Dorothy Sayers wrote 'Murder Must Advertise', and very few people have written a more entertaining or dramatic mystery story." —*The New Yorker*

Dorothy Stockbridge Tillet
(John Stephen Strange)

THE MAN WHO KILLED FORTESCUE

"Better than average." —*Saturday Review of Literature*

Henry Kitchell Webster

WHO IS THE NEXT? (available 5/81)

"A double murder, private-plane piloting, a neat impersonation, and a delicate courtship are adroitly combined by a writer who knows how to use the language." —Jacques Barzun and Wendell Hertig Taylor

Anna Mary Wells

MURDERER'S CHOICE (*available 4/81*)
"Good writing, ample action, and excellent character work."
—*Saturday Review of Literature*

A TALENT FOR MURDER (*available 4/81*)
"The discovery of the villain is a decided shock."
—*Books*

If you enjoyed this book you'll want to know about THE PERENNIAL LIBRARY MYSTERY SERIES

Nicholas Blake

☐	P 456	THE BEAST MUST DIE	$1.95
☐	P 427	THE CORPSE IN THE SNOWMAN	$1.95
☐	P 493	THE DREADFUL HOLLOW	$1.95
☐	P 397	END OF CHAPTER	$1.95
☐	P 419	MINUTE FOR MURDER	$1.95
☐	P 520	THE MORNING AFTER DEATH	$1.95
☐	P 521	A PENKNIFE IN MY HEART	$2.25
☐	P 531	THE PRIVATE WOUND	$2.25
☐	P 494	A QUESTION OF PROOF	$1.95
☐	P 495	THE SAD VARIETY	$2.25
☐	P 457	THE SMILER WITH THE KNIFE	$1.95
☐	P 428	THOU SHELL OF DEATH	$1.95
☐	P 418	THE WHISPER IN THE GLOOM	$1.95
☐	P 399	THE WIDOW'S CRUISE	$1.95
☐	P 400	THE WORM OF DEATH	$2.25

E. C. Bentley

☐	P 440	TRENT'S LAST CASE	$1.95
☐	P 516	TRENT'S OWN CASE	$2.25

Buy them at your local bookstore or use this coupon for ordering:

HARPER & ROW, Mail Order Dept. #PMS, 10 East 53rd St., New York, N.Y. 10022.

Please send me the books I have checked above. I am enclosing $ _____ which includes a postage and handling charge of $1.00 for the first book and 25¢ for each additional book. Send check or money order. No cash or C.O.D.'s please.

Name _____

Address _____

City _____ State _____ Zip _____

Please allow 4 weeks for delivery. USA and Canada only. This offer expires 1/1/82. Please add applicable sales tax.

Gavin Black

	P 473	A DRAGON FOR CHRISTMAS	$1.95
	P 485	THE EYES AROUND ME	$1.95
	P 472	YOU WANT TO DIE, JOHNNY?	$1.95

George Harmon Coxe

| | P 527 | MURDER WITH PICTURES | $2.25 |

Edmund Crispin

| | P 506 | BURIED FOR PLEASURE | $1.95 |

Kenneth Fearing

| | P 500 | THE BIG CLOCK | $1.95 |

Andrew Garve

	P 430	THE ASHES OF LODA	$1.50
	P 451	THE CUCKOO LINE AFFAIR	$1.95
	P 429	A HERO FOR LEANDA	$1.50
	P 449	MURDER THROUGH THE LOOKING GLASS	$1.95
	P 441	NO TEARS FOR HILDA	$1.95
	P 450	THE RIDDLE OF SAMSON	$1.95

Buy them at your local bookstore or use this coupon for ordering:

HARPER & ROW, Mail Order Dept. #PMS, 10 East 53rd St., New York, N.Y. 10022.
Please send me the books I have checked above. I am enclosing $ _____ which includes a postage and handling charge of $1.00 for the first book and 25¢ for each additional book. Send check or money order. No cash or C.O.D.'s please.

Name _____

Address _____

City _____ State _____ Zip _____
Please allow 4 weeks for delivery. USA and Canada only. This offer expires 1/1/82. Please add applicable sales tax.

Michael Gilbert

☐	P 446	BLOOD AND JUDGMENT	$1.95
☐	P 459	THE BODY OF A GIRL	$1.95
☐	P 448	THE DANGER WITHIN	$1.95
☐	P 447	DEATH HAS DEEP ROOTS	$1.95
☐	P 458	FEAR TO TREAD	$1.95

C. W. Grafton

☐	P 519	BEYOND A REASONABLE DOUBT	$1.95

Edward Grierson

☐	P 528	THE SECOND MAN	$2.25

Cyril Hare

☐	P 455	AN ENGLISH MURDER	$1.95
☐	P 522	TRAGEDY AT LAW	$2.25
☐	P 514	UNTIMELY DEATH	$1.95
☐	P 454	WHEN THE WIND BLOWS	$1.95
☐	P 523	WITH A BARE BODKIN	$2.25

Matthew Head

☐	P 541	THE CABINDA AFFAIR (available 6/81)	$2.25
☐	P 542	MURDER AT THE FLEA CLUB (available 6/81)	$2.25

Buy them at your local bookstore or use this coupon for ordering:

HARPER & ROW, Mail Order Dept. #PMS, 10 East 53rd St., New York, N.Y. 10022.

Please send me the books I have checked above. I am enclosing $ _____ which includes a postage and handling charge of $1.00 for the first book and 25¢ for each additional book. Send check or money order. No cash or C.O.D.'s please.

Name _____

Address _____

City _____ State _____ Zip _____

Please allow 4 weeks for delivery. USA and Canada only. This offer expires 1/1/82. Please add applicable sales tax.

M. V. Heberden

☐ P 533   ENGAGED TO MURDER $2.25

James Hilton

☐ P 501   WAS IT MURDER? $1.95

Elspeth Huxley

☐ P 540   THE AFRICAN POISON MURDERS
             (available 5/81) $2.25

Frances Iles

☐ P 517   BEFORE THE FACT $1.95
☐ P 532   MALICE AFORETHOUGHT $1.95

Lange Lewis

☐ P 518   THE BIRTHDAY MURDER $1.95

Arthur Maling

☐ P 482   LUCKY DEVIL $1.95
☐ P 483   RIPOFF $1.95
☐ P 484   SCHROEDER'S GAME $1.95

Austin Ripley

☐ P 387   MINUTE MYSTERIES $1.95

Buy them at your local bookstore or use this coupon for ordering:

Thomas Sterling

☐ P 529   THE EVIL OF THE DAY $2.25

Julian Symons

☐ P 468   THE BELTING INHERITANCE $1.95
☐ P 469   BLAND BEGINNING $1.95
☐ P 481   BOGUE'S FORTUNE $1.95
☐ P 480   THE BROKEN PENNY $1.95
☐ P 461   THE COLOR OF MURDER $1.95
☐ P 460   THE 31ST OF FEBRUARY $1.95

Dorothy Stockbridge Tillet
(John Stephen Strange)

☐ P 536   THE MAN WHO KILLED FORTESCUE $2.25

Henry Kitchell Webster

☐ P 539   WHO IS THE NEXT? (available 5/81) $2.25

Anna Mary Wells

☐ P 534   MURDERER'S CHOICE (available 4/81) $2.25
☐ P 535   A TALENT FOR MURDER (available 4/81) $2.25

Buy them at your local bookstore or use this coupon for ordering: